Black & White Trilogy

A Gay Shifter Romance MM

By: Jodie Sloan

Yap Kee Chong

8345 NW 66 ST #B7885

Miami, FL 33166

Createspace

Copyright 2014

Get Future New Releases In This Series For 99 Cents

http://eepurl.com/7jckT

Like Us On Facebook

https://www.facebook.com/pages/JodieSloan/180879798753822

Contents

FORBIDDEN PASSION

CHAPTER 1

School had finally come to an end and Tom was looking forward to the rest of his life. He was also looking forward to going to learn more about horses on the ranch. He had lived with them all his life, but he had never really learned as much as he wanted to learn about them. His father, Thomas Langley Sharpe II owned a ranch that specialized in rearing and training racehorses, but Tom had never had a proper chance to get close to the horses and learn much about them. He had always been too busy with his school work, even going for tuition during the vacations. He was now however free of that, and it excited him tremendously due to the fact that he was now joining the real world. He was also looking forward to becoming an excellent equestrian with the help of Valerie. Valerie had lived with them ever since he was a little child and Tom had grown fond of him in many different ways.

Valerie knew everything about Tom Langley Sharpe II's businesses and was his right hand man in running the estate. Tom had gotten a crush on Valerie when he was still sixteen, but Valerie had shown no interest in him, and so Tom had let it go. There was something within him that he could not understand, but Tom felt as if he was more into men than women. He found himself admiring men more and even found them a lot more attractive in a sexual way. He would find himself staring at a man's buttocks more than was necessary, and at times it even scared him, since there were not very many gay people in that part of the country. All of his friend's back in school ha been straight, but maybe Tom had become gay due to the fact that he had been practically brought up by Valerie, hanging around him and other men on the paddocks instead of being out in the city partying with the girls like most of the other young men his age.

"What are your plans for today?" his dad asked as they sat at the dining table having a late breakfast. "I'm pretty sure that you'll be bored hanging around the ranch, but you could ask Valerie to drive you into town to meet up with your friend's."

"No, dad, I think I'll just hang around the ranch, and besides, I want to get closer to my stallion, Eagle. You just bought her for me and I want to be there through the training programme," Tom said, placing his cup of tea onto the saucer. "Maybe over the weekend I can go into New Orleans to meet up with some of the boys."

"I think he has really grown into a mature boy now, Thomas, don't you think," his mother, Pricilla, regarding him above the rim of her glasses proudly.

"Yeah, he is definitely taking after my blood. That is a good thing, Jr., I would also like you to start learning to manage this estate, since it will one day all be yours. Your mother and I aren't going to be here forever, you know," Thomas said.

"Yes, dad, I've been thinking about that, and I think I'll start working with Valerie, since he pretty much knows all of the operations on the ranch. I think that it would be best for me to start from down up, that way I'll have a hands on experience on all of the nitty gritty involved," Tom said, wondering how fun it was going to be finally starting to learn of the operations of the ranch and putting some of his schooling into action.

"Perfect, you go ahead and let me know how it goes, and if there is anything that you need," his father said, getting up and patting him on the back on his way out of the kitchen.

"I'll do that, dad," Tom said, also getting up and pushing his chair back under the table. "I'll see you later, mom."

Tom went upstairs to his bedroom so that he could change into some suitable outdoor clothes. He was looking forward to spending time at the stables and the paddocks with Eagle, a white stallion that his father had gotten for him as a gift for his graduation from high school. It was a beautiful horse with a furry tail and hooves, one that Tom knew must have cost his father a pretty dime. Tom was the only child in the family and was therefore loved and pampered in ways that would make any other person jealous. His father could do anything for him provided that it made Tom happy. From the way that Tom had been brought up, he was not the type of person to take advantage of such kind gestures, only asking for what he really needed. He believed in hard work, honest and loyalty. The only thing that was missing in Tom's life was love, intimate love. He was yet to find that special person who could take his breath away whenever he saw them, and he was more than sure that it had to be a man, which only made things a lot more difficult, since it was hard to get men who were looking for men as lovers.

"Danny, it is so good to see you, it has been a while," he said to the dark skinned boy about his own age who worked at the stables, noting the way that Daniel seemed to have matured and blossomed into a handsome young man since they last met six months ago.

"I'm also very happy to see you, Master Tom," Daniel said, standing upright and holding the brim of his hat Don in respect.

"Danny, I don't want you calling me Master, you make me feel very old and colonial, just call me Tom, will you. We have known each other and been friends for years, and to me we are equals," Tom said, walking up to Daniel and hugging him warmly, a tremor passing through his body as their bodies touched, Daniel's masculine smell going straight to Tom's head and making him dizzy with a sudden surge of arousal. He pulled away from Daniel quickly when he felt his cock beginning to react inside his pants. "How have you been, my friend, and look at you, you have really grown since we last met."

"Well, Tom, thank you. Your dad has been feeding us very well here," he said, patting the white horse that he had been brushing down.

"I'm guessing that this is eagle, right, I've never seen this one here before?" Tom said excitedly, his attention quickly shifting to the horse, his admiration of Daniel temporarily forgotten.

"Yes, she is a true beauty, isn't she?" Daniel said, almost dreamily. "I've always dreamt of owning a horse of my own someday, you know. You are a very privileged guy, you should always be glad for that."

"You're right, Danny, and I'm gonna make you a promise, you have always been a very good friend to me, and I will do whatever is in my power to help you out. you are like the brother that I never had," Tom said.

Tom had known Daniel Peters since they were eight, when Daniel's parents had died and he had come to work at the ranch to make ends meet. Being the same age, they had immediately hit it off as good friends, and they would do many of the tasks together. Thomas Sr. had therefore brought Daniel to work at the house so that he could be closer to his son, who had no other company his own age. As Daniel grew older, becoming a teenager, he had to move to the stables where more hands were needed, and Tom was moved to a boarding school in the city. Despite spending so little time together, Tom and Daniel remained good friends and stayed in communication when they were apart. Tom treated Daniel as an equal and did not look at him as a black boy. Today, he could not believe just how handsome Daniel had become to the point of getting him turned on the way that he was right now.

"So, what are the plans for today, I wanna spend more time with the horse?" Tom asked, picking up a brush and beginning to rub it over the white mane.

"I was actually thinking of taking her to the tracks for some training," Daniel said, beginning to put away the buckets and brushes he had been using to clean the horse.

"Perfect, I'm coming with you."

They spent the whole morning at the tracks, and although Danny had become a very good horse trainer, Tom seemed to concentrate more on his looks. Danny was a muscular guy, and the fact that he was dressed in a tight fitting T shirt only made him even hotter. Tom wondered what Daniel would look like without his shirt on, heck, without his clothes on. He wondered what it would feel like running his hands over Danny's body, tracing his fingers over the curves of his muscles all the way down to his crotch. Tom wondered what it would feel like wrapping his fingers around Danny's cock and beginning to jerk it up and down, and how Daniel would react. Just picturing his fingers wrapped around Danny's chocolate colored manhood made his own dick begin to get aroused again, and Tom had to divert his attention elsewhere so that he could remain sane.

CHAPTER 2

Daniel Peters looked at his friend Thomas Langley Sharpe III. He had changed quite a lot since the last time that they had met, and Daniel could not help but notice just how sexy he looked. It was a pity that even if he thought of him as sexy, getting into any sort of sexual relationship with him was completely out of the way. Tom would never approve of it, and Thomas Sr. might even end up firing him if he caught wind of such a thing. Daniel wondered why Tom kept stealing strange glances at him, even blushing when Danny caught him once. It was probably because they had not seen each other in a long time, although Danny hoped desperately that it was because he was also attracted to him. he had noticed the constant erection in Danny's pants too, but it was probably because he was looking forward to boning some hot chick in town.

Daniel wondered how the white cock would feel and taste in his mouth. Judging from the awesome size, Danny knew that he would have a hard time getting the whole cock into his mouth, but he could imagine how Tom's precum would taste. He had never made love to another man before, but Daniel had tasted his own secretions, which made him wonder if Tom's would taste the same. Anyway, those were just his thoughts because they were forbidden and almost taboo in action. He concentrated on his job, training the horse despite the fact that he was with Tom the whole time, which made it almost impossible not to. By the time that they went their separate ways for lunch, Daniel was feeling so horny, he went straight to his cabin and locked himself inside.

Taking off his clothes, he went into the bathroom and got the water running into the tub. His cock was rock hard as he got into the bath tub, the hot water only intensifying his arousal. He soaped up his hand and then wrapped his fingers around the thickness of his dick, beginning to jerk it up and down. Leaning back in the tub, Daniel closed his eyes thinking of Tom as he jerked his pecker. He imagined himself licking and sucking the head of Tom's dick, tasting him and relishing his delicious taste. Daniel even imagined Tom's hardness deep inside his butt hole, pushing in and out of it pleasurably as Tom held him by the hips from behind. Daniel felt the heat within his balls beginning to heighten, and he knew that he was almost reaching his climax. He gripped his dick tighter, jerking it faster and harder as he played his thumb over the tip pleasurably. Just as Tom's cock stiffened and exploded into his butt hole, spitting his hot load of cum deep within Daniel's buttocks, his shaft stiffened in his hand and erupted like a volcano, his creamy release shooting out of the slit and into the water. Daniel groaned as he jerked his dick furiously, feeling the explosion rocking him to the very core of his being.

CHAPTER 3

It had been a week since Tom had come back home, and each day he found himself daydreaming about Danny, but not in the normal way, in the erotic sort of way. He wondered how he was going to make it through the afternoon since they were on their way to stream on the ranch to let the horses drink water as they swam. It had been a favorite place of theirs since they were kids, and they would sneak there to swim. It was also a place where there was no disturbance from the ranch hands and other staff around the ranch, and they would do whatever they wanted there. Tom was riding Eagle, while Danny rode one of the other horses from the stable, and they were driving a heard of horses there.

"This place holds very fond memories for me, remember the time when we found a snake hanging on that branch hanging just over the stream?" Tom said, thinking back to their childhood.

"You were totally freaked out dude," Daniel laughed as he hoped off his horse and tethered it to a tree.

"Look who is laughing, you ran nonstop all the way back to the house, at least I stoned it," Tom replied, watching the horses drinking water as he disembarked from his horse.

"Well, I'm going in for a swim," Daniel said as he peeled of his shirt swiftly, tossing it onto the grass.

Tom felt his blood coming to a boil as he watched Daniel unbuckling the belt before pulling the button and zipper of his Jean's open. He slid the jeans down along with his boxers, and there was the sexiest scene that Tom had ever seen. One could think that Daniel hit the gym pretty often because of his well-toned muscles that even made Tom a little green with envy. Moving his eyes over Danny's body, Tom brought his eyes to rest on the part of Danny's body that interested him the most, his penis. It was limp, but Tom could already imagine how it would look like when it was fully blown and ready for action. It had a smooth dark head that looked tasty, making Tom imagine how it would feel penetrating him in his mouth and his butt hole. The dark patch of pubic hair was cut short and neat, and his balls hang loosely under the cock. Tom swallowed hard as he looked at the dick, almost as if he could not believe what he was seeing. He felt his own cock stifling in his pants as arousal began to course through his body.

"Tom, you are staring at my privates," Daniel said, turning away from Tom as Tom blushed deeply, his face filled with embarrassment. "Are you okay, sir?"

"I'm sorry, Danny, I just haven't been around another naked man in a while, and I guess I got carried away," he replied, tossing his Stetson to the ground and beginning to remove his shirt.

Moments later, both of the men were naked, and they ran into the water, splashing around as if they were ten years old again. At some point as they played in the water, chasing after each other under the water, Daniel swam right up directly infront of Tom, Danny's hand flicking over Tom's cock by mistake. Tom felt a jolt of power surging through his body, almost like some electric current, and his cock began to get hard under the water. Daniel stood directly infront of tom, their bodies an inch away from each other, and both men looked at each other in the eyes. Tom was not sure if that was fire that he saw in Danny's eyes, because it looked as if there was a flame burning deep in them, reflecting the one in his own eyes. Goosebumps formed on his forearms as the two men began moving their heads slowly together, almost as if there was some sort of magnetic pull drawing them together. Their lips touched lightly at first, and then they crushed onto each other hard as Tom and Danny began kissing hungrily. Black lips fused over white lips, and Tom parted his lips gently, allowing the sweet invasion of his tongue into Danny's mouth.

Their bodies pressed hard together, and Tom realized that Danny had a hard on just as hard as his as the dicks rubbed over each other. Unable to resist the urge, Tom pushed his hand under the water, pressing it in between them and taking his hand down to the dark monster cock. Tom was trembling with desire as he wrapped his fingers around Daniel's thickness and began jerking it up and down slowly, just like he had dreamed of the past few days. Despite the coolness of the stream water, the cock was hot and hard, and it made Tom's blood rush through his veins as arousal like he had never experienced before pulsated through his body. Danny began moving his hips back and forth, his dick beginning to move inside the fingers around it, and Tom felt as if he would explode when he felt Danny moaning into his mouth. Their lips were fused together tightly, and Tom had the feeling that this was how they were meant to be for the rest of their lives. He opened his eyes to look at Daniel just to make sure that this was actually happening and not one of the numerous dreams that he got every night.

As they kissed, Daniel reached his hand behind Tom, squeezing his butt deliciously and then pushed Tom's butt into himself, their bodies pressing even tighter together. Tom felt as if he was drunk with desire, and the heat of the summer sun on their bodies only seemed to heighten that. Tom felt Daniel's hand parting his butt cheeks, and moments later, Danny ran his finger up and down the length of the crack, bringing it to a stop against the rim of his ass hole. Tom breathed in deeply when he felt the finger pushing deliciously into his butt hole, Danny pushing it in slowly and stopping every few inches to let Tom's butt get used to the new intrusion. Tom had never felt anything like that before, the feel of the finger rubbing against his hymen. It was the most adorable sensation that he had ever felt in his life and he knew that he would always be addicted to it from now onwards. Danny began moving the finger in and out of Tom's butt hole, finger fucking him and driving him crazy with desire.

Tom felt the heat within his balls coming to a boil and making his dick even harder. He was jerking his cock against Danny's thigh in the water, and it was the most sensational feeling of his life. The way that they were holding and pleasuring each other so naturally was a clear indication to Tom that they were indeed made for each other. Danny was breathing heavily, his whole body filled with desire, while his chest was pressed against Tom's, and Tom could almost swear that he could hear their hearts beating in symphony. Tom was still reeling in the desire that was being given to him when Daniel suddenly pulled his finger out of his anus and his lips and body away from Tom, his face suddenly filled with shame.

"I'm really sorry about that, Tom, I don't know what came over me," he said, his eyes avoiding Tom's as he turned to look away from him.

Tom blushed, suddenly overcome by guilt although he regretted why Danny had pulled away just at the height of their passion. He wished that it could continue forever right there in the stream with just nature as their only audience. His body was still boiling with desire, almost as if he was a dog on heat, and his cock was harder and more aroused than ever, although this was all probably a big mistake, something forbidden that could never be. He could still feel the effect of Danny's finger in his butt hole, and he desperately wanted it back in there, or better still, his dark hard monster cock, pummeling his opening with desire, a desire that can only be felt between two men in love.

"It's not your fault, Danny. We are both adults, and I think that we were just overcome by sudden emotions that were beyond our control," Tom said quickly, hoping that Danny did not regret and blame himself for what had happened.

"I think it was all my fault, I have been through a long dry spell, and maybe it is time that I went into town and got myself a lass to take away the lust within," Danny said, the words driving a sword through Tom's heart and piercing it in the core.

"Come on, let's get the horses back to the stables, the other ranch hands will come looking for us very soon," Tom said, deciding to change the topic and wading out of the water despite his still fully erect shaft.

He noted the way that Danny stared at him hungrily, almost as if he wanted to pounce on him already and pursue the passion that they had began in the water. Danny got out of the water behind Tom, and through the side of his eye, Tom noticed for the first time how his dark skinned friend's cock looked when it was hard, and it looked more delicious than chocolate in many ways. There was no way that he was ever going to be able to get that picture out of his mind for the rest of his life.

CHAPTER 4

It had been months since the incident at the stream, but for Daniel it was still fresh in his mind, almost as if it had happened yesterday. He recalled the way that his finger had felt penetrating Tom's butt hole, and every time that he remembered that, it made him get a hard on. The hole had been tight and God only knew how it would feel if it was his cock doing the penetration instead.

"Daniel, Mr. Thomas and Master Tom would like to see you at the mansion," Clyde, one of the ranch hands at the farm popped his head into Daniel's shack.

"Thanks, Clyde, any idea what it is all about?" Danny asked, wondering why in the world they needed him at the mansion on a Sunday, since it was usually his day off and he liked spending it day dreaming of Tom and his hot sexy body.

"I'm not sure, but I saw a truck bringing in a black Arabian stallion very similar to Master Tom's. They probably want you to take charge of it, mate, go on, hurry up," the short guy said, closing the door.

Daniel changed into his working clothes and boots, and then grabbing his Stetson, he hurried off to the ranch house, which was a short distance away from his quarters. Things had changed quite a bit since Tom had come back from school, and Danny had been moved away from the other staff quarters located on the far end of the ranch and been brought closer to the ranch house. The other ranch hands considered him very privileged and could not understand why. Thomas Sr. was determined to make him happy and as comfortable as possible since he was his sons best friend, and Danny did not know how he would ever be able to pay back the kindness. He was also now a full time horse trainer and was in charge of all the other trainers, the only other staff member above him being Valerie, the soft spoken Frenchman who managed the estate alongside its owners, and Mr. Thomas Sr.'s right hand man. Valerie had also sort of acted as a father to him after the death of his parents, and Daniel would forever be indebted to him for that. Valerie trained Tom and Daniel martial arts skills almost every morning before the sun came out, and the young men had both become very good at both fighting and spurring.

CHAPTER 5

Thomas Langley Sharpe II regarded the dark young man as he approached the mansion. He was standing by the window of his study and had decided to get the young man a gift that his son had mentioned. It was meant to be a surprise for both young men, and he was hoping that it would make them both happy. They were now both 18 and this was going to be just one of his gifts to them. Valerie had told him about Tom being a gay oriented young man, and had even told him of the way that Tom and Daniel looked at each other. It was evident that they were both madly in love with each other but too proud to admit it, or probably scared of what other people would think. Thomas was ready to do anything for his son just to see him happy, and he had watched Daniel growing up and come to like him. He was well mannered, very respectful and also very intelligent. If his son was in love with him, Thomas was not going to get into the way, instead he was going to make it a lot easier for the young men to discover their love and make it blossom.

Pricilla, Tom's mother did not like the idea very much and was looking forward to seeing Tom with a wife and kids of his own, but Thomas bluffed her off, saying that Tom's happiness came first. If he wanted a wife and family at some stage of his life, he could always get one, but right now he was still young and had the right to enjoy it and discover what made him happy. He moved away from the window when he saw Valerie greeting Daniel and welcoming him into the house, making his way downstairs to meet the young man and his son.

"Good morning, Danny, I'm sorry to bother you on a Sunday morning because I understand that this is your day off, but what I have to show you could not wait," he said to Daniel as he walked into the foyer.

"That is not a problem at all, Mr. Thomas," Danny said, removing his Stetson and bowing his head forward slightly.

"Dad, I heard that you wanted to see us," Tom said, bounding down the stairs to join Thomas and Daniel in the foyer.

"Yes, Tom, there is something that I wanted to show both of you," he said, leading them to the kitchen and out the back door of the house, heading towards the stables.

"Dad, why are you sounding so mysterious, what are you up to?" Tom asked, looking from his father to Danny questioningly as they followed Thomas Sr.

"Relax, my son, there is nothing wrong, and there is no mystery about it," Thomas said as they walked into the stables. "It is just a little surprise that I have for your friend here."

"Me?" Daniel said questioningly as he looked at Thomas with equal curiosity that Tom also had.

"Well," Thomas said as they came to a stop outside one of the stables, the young men too encompassed with curiosity to notice the Arabian stallion in the stable. "You two are now adults, and Daniel has been very good to us. I would like to treat him as my son, and I would like you two to become even closer. I have therefore bought him a gift so that you two can be equal, this here is Destiny."

Both men suddenly noticed the cute lady standing in the stable, looking at them with graceful brown eyes, and Tom's jaw dropped. Her coat was dark, almost like the night, and she was very furry just like Eagle and their color their only difference. Thomas looked at the young men, and he could read the joy in their eyes.

"Mr. Thomas, I don't know what to say..." Daniel said, looking as if he could not believe what he was seeing. "Is she really-"

"Yes, Daniel, she is yours, so that you can ride around with Tom. Take it as a gift for turning into a nice young man, and there are more gifts in the making, you will both begin going for your driving lessons. I am sponsoring both of you because I have confidence that you will both make excellent drivers," Thomas said proudly.

"Really, dad, you are the best dad that there is in this world," Tom said, throwing his hands around his dad's shoulders and giving him a bear hug.

"I don't know how I will ever be able to thank you, Mr. Thomas, this is all like some sort of dream because I would never have been able to achieve any of this on my own," Daniel said as tears stung his eyes and began trickling down his cheeks freely.

"It is okay, my boy, you have always been like a son to me, and besides, you are my only child's best friend, which makes it only fair if you are equal. I want you to call me Thomas, or dad, don't use the Mr. thing, it is way too official for what we have here," Thomas said, holding Daniel an arm's length away and looking into his dark mysterious eyes, eyes that his son looked into with passion.

CHAPTER 6

Riding around the ranch had become a lot more fun because of the fact that Danny now had his own horse, which he was very proud of. Tom still found it very hard to believe that his dad had actually bought for Danny the stallion and was even paying for his driving lessons too. It had brought them much closer together, although there was still some tension between them when they remembered what had happened between them at the stream.

"Time really flies, huh, I can't believe that we will soon be going for the driving test, I'm sure that the DMV will approve our licenses," Tom said, slowing Eagle down from a gallop as Danny caught up with him at the end of the tracks.

"Yeah, that is one hell of a huge milestone that we are going to achieve, and it is all thanks to your dad, Tom, I think you have the greatest dad in the world," Danny said as they began riding towards the stables.

"I'll agree on that, and I think that he is also your dad too, I mean, he has even allowed you to move into the mansion with us, and you have your own wing," Tom replied, swinging his leg over the horse as he disembarked, handing the reins to a handler.

"Well, we had better hurry up, we don't want to be late for the driving tests, we need to get there before most of the other people do," Daniel said as they walked to the house.

Tom went to his bedroom quickly and removed his clothes, dashing to the shower for a quick bath. He then changed into casual clothes, a brown polo shirt and black pants, topped off with black loafers. He then made his way out of the bedroom, grabbing a jacket from the walk in wardrobe. He decided to pass through Danny's room to see if he was ready to go, and so branched off into his wing of the house. Without bothering to knock, he opened the door and entered the bedroom. Danny was still in the bathroom, and so Tom decided to make himself comfortable on the bed, flipping through a magazine that he found on the dresser. As he began flipping through the magazine, Tom realized that it was a gay magazine and full of male porn pictures. Suddenly feeling aroused, Tom began paying a little more attention to the magazines. It looked like Danny was into gay porn, and Tom felt a pang of guilt passing through him when he imagined Danny with another man other than him.

His cock was soon rock hard as he continued flipping through the pages, noting that none of the cocks in the images looked half as sexy and arousing as Danny's chocolate dick. A few minutes later, Tom heard the bathroom door opening, and he quickly flipped the magazine closed and tossed it onto the dresser, pretending that nothing had happened as Danny walked into the room stark naked, his sheer nakedness the epitome of beauty. His body was still wet making him look even sexier than ever, and Tom's eyes shot to Daniel's crotch, checking out his limp cock and swallowing hard when he remembered the way that it had felt against his thigh when it was hard. It took all of his will power not to walk over to Danny and take his dark penis into his hand, massaging it until it became hard and then taking it into his mouth and beginning to suck on the head. It was almost as if God had taken his time when he was sculpting Danny and Tom was sure that there would never be another man who had such an effect on him the way that Danny affected him.

"Tom, you showered pretty quickly," Danny said, tossing a towel onto the bed and walking into his wardrobe as Tom's eyes followed him hungrily.

"I generally shower very quickly," Tom answered slowly. "And we don't have very much time, by the time that Valerie drives us into New Orleans it will already be an hour."

"I guess you are right," Danny said walking back out of the wardrobe with his pants and shoes on, and buttoning up his shirt.

The scent of his maleness and his cologne made Tom feel dizzy with desire, imagining what it would feel like mingled with his own. He got up from the bed and began making his way to the door, glad that his erection had cooled off even though he was still burning with desire.

"I'll be downstairs when you are ready," Tom said, quickly exiting Danny's room, scared of what he might do, although now more than ever he knew that Danny was into gay stuff, which made the possibilities of a relationship come alive.

By the time that he got down the stairs, Tom had convinced himself that he was going to find time and tell Daniel exactly how he felt about him. It was either now or never, or Tom could risk losing the only person that he loved to someone else. He decided that he would do it tomorrow since it was a weekend, and things would be a lot slower with their schedules. He was going to have to figure out a way to break the news of how he felt about Daniel to him.

"Well, here I am, we had better get going," Daniel said, taking the stairs two at a time.

They set off for the driving test ten minutes later.

CHAPTER 7

Saturday morning was tense for Tom because he still had not figured out what he was going to tell Danny. He was however very happy because of the fact that Danny and he had both passed the driving tests and their licenses were approved. It was the best thing to happen that week, and they could not wait to tell his dad the news. They were more than sure that he too would be elated, and especially since he had placed such confidence in them. Thomas and Pricilla had gone out of town on a business weekend and would be back tomorrow, which was just fine because Tom intended to spend as much time with Daniel, alone. He paced his room, wondering where all of his creativity had gone since he could not seem to get what to say to Daniel, and neither did he seem to have the guts. He walked over to the mirror to double check how he looked. He was dressed in tight fitting blue jeans, a khaki shirt and riding boots, excellent clad for a day on the prairie.

Yes, that was it, they could go riding on the prairie on the far end of the ranch which was deserted and would probably have cattle. He had not been there in a long time, and Tom realized that it was the best place to take Danny and propose to him without any prying eyes or anything. They could camp out there until tomorrow, which could actually make it even more exciting. Who knows, they might even make love the whole night. Thinking of that, Tom felt excitement coursing through his veins as he imagined Danny's dark lips wrapped around his cock, doing forbidden things to it. "Yes', Tom said aloud, throwing his fist in the air.

"Somebody sure seems to be in a good mood today," Danny said, walking into the bedroom unexpectedly.

"You can say that again. When was the last time that you went camping, Daniel?" Tom turned to look at his dark skinned prince.

"I can't even remember, I think when we were eleven down by the Mississippi, remember. That time when the fish was too heavy for us to reel it in and Valerie had to come to our aid," Daniel said, a dreamy look coming onto his face.

"You wanna know what I was thinking?" Tom said excitedly. "I was thinking that maybe we could go camping today, you know, to the prairie or something. We could pitch tent there, build a bonfire and drink beer, how does that sound?"

"I think that is a great idea, why haven't we ever thought about doing something like that?" Daniel said, and Tom noted the way that he too seemed to become excited at the idea.

"I guess that we were too busy becoming adults to think of it, come on, we had better start making the arrangements. It is going to be an almost three hour ride and we need to get there on time to catch some tuna in the river there," Tom said, leading the way out of the bedroom.

They had Anita, the cook, pack for them food that they would need and then drove into town to purchase new tents and sleeping bags. Tom thought of how ironical it was for them to buy two tents and sleeping bags and yet he intended to seduce Danny and probably wind up making love to him in one tent the whole night. The moment that they got back to the ranch, they put whatever they would need on some extra horses and then set off. It was a good thing that the horses were in top form and so they did not have to keep stopping to rest. They stopped once to give them a drink in one of the pools along the way. It was mid afternoon by the time that they found a good spot on the prairie where they could pitch tent.

"I must say, the heat today is intense," Tom said, hoping off his horse and peeling off his polo shirt.

CHAPTER 8

Daniel looked at Tom's tanned chest as he removed his shirt. Hot indeed it was, but not only because of the heat. Danny felt as if he had pent up desire that was burning to explode. His balls felt as if they were on fire as he wondered how camping was going to be. He was not very sure if he was going to be able to resist his hot and handsome friend, since just looking at him made Danny feel like melting within.

"Yeah, it is a good thing that most of the way we were riding in the trees. Let's set up camp and then let the horses graze a little while we go fishing, how does that sound?" Daniel said, also reaching for his T shirt and pulling it off swiftly to remain bare chested like Tom.

"That is the perfect plan, in this warm weather the tuna are bound to be where the water is slightly deeper, where it is cool," Tom said as they began unloading their things from the other two horses.

They went ahead and set up their camp, erecting their tents and collecting firewood. When they were satisfied that everything was in order, they released their horses to graze, glad that the ranch was in paddocks and the horses could not go too far off.

"I think I'll carry a couple of bottles of beer to keep us company as we fish," Tom said, reaching for two six packs.

Daniel noted the way that Tom's muscles flexed deliciously as he carried the beers out of the supply tent. How he longed to ran his fingers over those biceps, tracing every line of muscle and doing other things that were dangerously delicious. The beers would be good because they would take away that awkward feeling that they kept getting when they were alone ever since the incident at the stream.

"Yeah, that is an excellent idea, I'll get the lines and the mats," Danny replied.

They began their short trek to the river, which was not very far off. Danny pulled the brim of his Stetson down over his eyes to shade off the afternoon sun as he followed Tom down the trail that led to the river. When they got to the river, they located a nice spot from where they could fish, and where the water seemed a little deep. They laid their mats on the ground and pitched their hooks into the water before settling Don on the mats and popping open a beer each.

"I feel as if I'm 11 all over again, only, with a beer in my hand," Tom said as he lay back on his mat, planting one hand behind his head as the other one clung to his bottle of beer.

"Yeah, it has been a while since we did anything like this," Danny said, leaning on his elbow and regarding his friend, his eyes roving over Tom's body, practically undressing him and leaving him stark naked to begin making love to him.

Daniel was sure that he saw a movement in Tom's pants sparking off his interest. His cock was slowly coming alive, a tent beginning to form in his pants although Tom seemed to have totally ignored it. Daniel felt his own arousal coming alive within him as a now familiar burning sensation engulfed his crotch. Maybe it was the heat that was making Tom's dick become hard, or maybe he was thinking of his girlfriend, but it was turning Daniel on in ways that he had never imagined possible. He felt his own dick beginning to get hard despite him trying to will it to stop. It was as if the manhood had a brain of its own and would not listen to his brains logic, because within seconds, it was as hard as a rock and rearing for some action.

"Danny, there is something that has been on my mind, and I wanted to let you know before it is too late," Tom said, taking a swig of his beer as Danny wondered what he had to say to him.

"You can tell me anything, Tom, I'm your friend," Danny sat up, crossing his legs under him and leaning forward to hide his erection.

"That is just the thing, Danny, I wanna be more than just friends with you…. I don't really know how to say it…" Tom faltered.

"Say whatever is on your mind," Danny said, more attentive now than ever, and not very sure if he'd heard right.

"Well, the thing is that deep down inside me, I've had these feelings that I can't quite understand, Danny. I think I'm in love," Tom said, looking up at Danny. "I'm in love with you, Danny, and I was hoping that maybe you could give me a small spot in your heart."

"I've always loved you right from the time that I came to work on this ranch, and you will always have a place in my heart, Tom, you are my best friend," Danny said, thinking that Tom probably meant the friendship kind of love.

"That is not what I meant, Danny," Tom said, getting up and crawling over to Danny's mat. "I meant like this."

Before Danny could think and process what was going on, Tom's lips came crushing onto his, white skin blending with dark skin as they began kissing passionately and even hungrily. Danny felt himself melting into Tom as his lips parted, allowing Tom's tongue a delicious entry into his mouth. Their tongues began rubbing over each other, tasting each other in the most intimate ways, the fishing job totally forgotten. Danny felt as if all of his desire had come erupting to the surface, and Tom pushed him onto his back on the mat as they kissed like there was no tomorrow. Tom lay on him partially, and Danny could feel the hardness of Tom's dick pressed against his thigh. Tom moved his hand over Danny's chest, pushing it through the waist of his pants and taking it all the way to his cock.

Danny was aching with need as Tom wrapped his fingers around the pecker and began jerking it up and down slowly, holding it firmly as if it belonged to him.

Danny had never felt such arousal washing over him, and he moaned into Tom's mouth, his desire overwhelming him. Tom jerked his dick for a couple of minutes before he pulled his hand out of Danny's pants and pulled his lips away from Danny's, looking him deep in the eyes.

"I wanna see you naked, Danny, take off your clothes because I know that you want this too," Tom said to Danny, getting up and beginning to unbutton his own shirt, pulling it off swiftly.

"Tom…" was all that Danny could manage to get out of his desire filled haze as he got up and peeled off his T shirt.

He then went ahead and unbuckled his belt, pulling it off before pulling his pants open and letting them fall to the ground. As he took off his boxers, he looked at Tom only to realize that Tom had already removed all of his clothes and was standing looking at him with the most delicious looking hard on. As soon as Danny had kicked off his boxers, he moved infront of Tom and crouched infront of him, his hands going to Tom's dick and wrapping his fingers around it. He moved his head closer to the pecker and sniffed it in, the male scent making him feel dizzy with desire. Moving even closer, Danny stuck out his tongue and flicked it over the tip of the cock, getting a taste of the delicious precum that had already pooled over the slit. Tom groaned with pleasure as Danny rubbed his tongue over the tip of the cock, loving the salty male taste of the love juices, before Danny took the whole head of the pecker into his mouth and began sucking on it. He jerked the base of the dick as he began taking more and more of the dick into his mouth, swishing his tongue over the soft sensitive skin.

"Oh fuck, yeah, that feels good," Danny groaned as he brought his hand down onto Tom's head, pressing it harder onto his manhood and forcing more of the male meat into his mouth.

The thickness of Tom's dick strained against Danny's jaw uncomfortably, but Danny was determined to give Tom a good time. He had never given a blowjob before, but he did his best to suck on the dick as deliciously as he could, and from the way that Tom was breathing heavily, Danny could tell that he was getting it done right. He finally felt the thickness of the head pushing into his throat, and as he deep throated it, Danny gagged on the dick. He pulled his mouth off the dick, and as he stood up, Tom pulled him into his arms, fusing their lips together as they began kissing deeply. Danny wondered how Tom felt tasting the juices from his cock in Danny's mouth. His own dick was aching with need, an intense need to release and as he began rubbing it over Tom's thigh, Tom pulled his lips away from his and crouched down infront of him, taking Danny's cock into his mouth and beginning to suck on it.

Danny moaned out in pleasure when he felt Tom's tongue rubbing over his sensitive skin, erotic pleasure weaving its way through his body. He felt as if all that was happening was a dream and he pinched himself just to make sure that it was actually happening. He then looked down at the way his dark length was being sucked on, taking his hands down to Tom's brown hair and combing his fingers through it as he held Mike's head firmly and pushed his dick into his mouth. He started driving his dark snake in and out of Tom's mouth, mouth fucking him as the cock went deeper and deeper into his mouth. He did it gently, careful not to hurt his new found lover, and he felt the heat within his balls coming to a boil. He closed his eyes, savoring the intense pleasure that he was feeling, and within no time, he felt his dick stiffening as a huge load of cum erupted from it, filling Tom's mouth. Shot after shot of semen filled his mouth and Danny opened his eyes to look at the way Tom was struggling to swallow all of it, although some still managed to make its way out through the corners of his mouth. Danny had never in his life had a release so great, and he felt as if it had taken all of his strength away.

Danny quickly stood up, locking his mouth over Tom's and kissing him, giving him a generous amount of semen. The taste of his own cum was new to him, but being that it was coming from Tom, Danny loved it and did not know if he would ever be able to get enough of it. His dick softened, but he could feel Tom's cock still as hard and aroused as ever and he knew that Tom was also dying for a release.

CHAPTER 9

Nothing had tasted more delicious than the cum he had just swallowed, and he could not believe the intensity of Danny's orgasm. His own arousal was driving him crazy with desire, and he longed to also have a similar climax or even better. He pulled his mouth away from Tom's reluctantly and looked at Daniel deep in the eyes. In the brown eyes, Tom could see more than just passion and intimacy in there, there was a deep and intense passion filled love that reflected the one in his own eyes. Danny moved away from Tom and turned around slowly, looking at Tom directly in the eyes as he displayed his buttocks for Tom to see. Tom swallowed hard when he saw Danny's dark ass looking at him welcomingly, and his cock twitched at the thought of penetrating Danny's butt hole.

Tom crouched down behind Danny and parted Danny's butt cheeks wide open as Danny leaned forward. His butt hole was dark and Tom moved his face closer to it, running his tongue over the butt crack and bringing it to a stop on the rim of the butt hole. Spitting on the butt hole, he started pushing a finger into it, driving it in slowly and stopping every now and then to let the butt hole get used to the new intrusion. Tom pushed the finger all the way in and then began pushing and pulling it in and out of the ass hole, finger fucking Danny. Danny was unable to conceal his pleasure, moaning softly as the finger ploughed in and out of the butt.

"Make love to me, Tom, I want to feel the hardness of your cock deep inside me, and the heat of your cum as you explode within," Danny said, turning to look back at Tom, who immediately pulled his finger out of the hole and stood up.

Parting the butt cheeks with one hand, he used his other one to guide his dick into the rim of the butt hole, the tip piercing into the crack. Tom pushed his dick in slowly, stopping after every few inches to let the butt get used to the new thickness. It felt tight and sweet against his dick, and Tom actually felt like slamming it in and fucking Daniel like there was no tomorrow, but he took his time since he did not want to make Daniel feel pain or uncomfortable. When the dick was fully inserted into the ass hole, Tom held Daniel by the hips and began pumping his cock in and out of it. It felt deliciously tight against his shaft, just the way that he had always imagined it. He looked at the way his white cock was drilling Danny's chocolate colored butt, and it was the most erotic thing that he had ever seen. Each thrust became harder and faster, and within no time, he erupted into an orgasm.

"Oh yeah, I'm coming," he groaned as the first shot of load erupted from his cock into Daniel's butt hole.

He pushed his dick hard into Daniel's ass hole, holding him tightly by the hips as spurt after spurt of his hot fluid drained into Danny. Never in his life had he ever felt anything so intense before, and he was glad that he had made the decision to tell Danny exactly how he felt. This was the best thing that had ever happened to him, and he would never regret his decision. When he was done coming, he finally pulled his softening cock out of Danny's butt and collapsed onto the mat.

"Thank you, Daniel, you don't know how long I have dreamt of this moment," he said softly.

"Me too, Tom, I just never knew how to bring it up, and I was not sure if you were into this sort of thing. I thought you probably had a girlfriend out there somewhere," Daniel said, sitting on the mat beside Tom and looking at his cum stained cock which was a contrast from the hard monster that had just shagged him.

"Hey, we have dinner to catch, and a long night of passionate love making after that," Tom said, sitting up and shifting his attention to his fishing rod.

CHAPTER 10

It had been a mind boggling weekend camping that Tom knew he would never forget. He had even wished that they could remain camping there forever, but there were things that needed to be attended to at home. Danny and he had decided that they would keep their relationship a secret, at least for the time being just in case Tom's parents were not very comfortable with gay relationships, although Tom had no reason he could think of that would make them object. They rode up to the stables and Tom noted that his parents had not yet come back from the trip because their car was not in the garage.

"Well, here we are, and it looks as if the old folks have not yet come home," he said, climbing off his horse and handing the reins to a handler as he winked at Daniel, a naughty grin on his face. "I'm pretty sure you know what that means."

"I guess we have the whole house to ourselves. Are you still going for the taekwondo competition in town this afternoon?" Daniel asked as they made their way to the house.

"I'm the defending champion, which means that I will have to be there to defend the title again," Tom replied, disappointment forming in his mind when he remembered the tournament in the afternoon.

"Welcome back home, sir," Anita said as they sauntered into her kitchen. "How was your camping trip, did it go well?"

"Very well, Anita, it was much better than we had anticipated, thank you," Tom said, hugging their elderly cook warmly before proceeding upstairs to his room.

He took a quick shower and then dressed into appropriate clothes for the tournament. It was going to be held from two, but Tom wanted to be ready for it by the time that it arrived, and so he wanted to go there right away. Grabbing the bag with his team's uniform, he dashed back down the stairs hoping to grab a quick light lunch. Just as he was rounding a corner into the living room, he bumped into Daniel, their bodies practically crushing, and the mere scent of his new lover reminded him of the hot weekend that they had just shared. Daniel held him by the back before he could fall, pulling him into himself, their faces barely an inch from each other. Without thinking twice, Tom pushed his lips over Daniel's, kissing him passionately as a now familiar flame lit up in his pants.

Daniel pushed his tongue deep into Tom's mouth, rubbing it over Tom's tongue erotically as the kiss became even more heated. Tom felt Daniel's dick hardening in his pants against his thigh, just the same way that his own was also blowing up and getting harder than ever. Tom knew that if he did not pull away from Daniel quickly, he might never make it out of the house today, and so he quickly pulled his lips away from Danny's dark sweet lips.

"If I continue kissing you I might end up losing the championship this season," he breathed heavily, moving back and looking around quickly to see if anyone had spotted them, particularly Anita.

"That was just a good luck kiss, honey, and I'm gonna be there with you, I wanna see you beating the hell out of your opponents," Daniel smiled at him sweetly.

"That will be a good thing because it will really inspire me knowing that you are there with me. Are you ready, I was hoping to grab a sandwich and leave," Tom said, slapping Daniel across his back.

"I'm good to go, I also just took a quick shower. Look at how hard your cock already is," Daniel said, wrapping his fingers around Tom's dick over the material of the pants he was wearing and squeezing it gently.

"You are the one who made it become like that, and so you are the one who is going to have to take care of it in the car on our way into town," Tom said, adjusting his cock in his pants so that the erection was not so visible and then pulling his short down to cover it.

Twenty minutes later, they were in Tom's new truck heading into town with Tom at the wheel and Daniel on the passenger seat. They had managed to tuck in a couple of Anita's cheese and ham sandwiches each and fresh fruit juice, and Tom felt that he was ready for the match. Valerie had done a good job at training him in various martial arts skills from the time that he was a small child, and now he was one of the best that there was in the city, having held the Junior championship cup for two years running. His parents had also been very supportive during the tournaments and now more than ever he needed to win this. It was the first time that Daniel was coming to watch him at a professional tournament, and there was no way that he was going to lose infront of him.

"You're rather quiet, worried about the games?" Daniel interrupted his thoughts.

"Not really, I'm actually looking forward to the tournament, it should be a piece of cake. Valerie pushed me really hard last week with the training, unless you have forgotten," Tom said, looking at Daniel briefly before putting his concentration back on the road.

"I really have confidence in you, and you can always count on my support even if there is nobody to else to do so. It is a pity Valerie had to miss this one, what did he go to do in town anyway, unless he has a lover or something there, I mean, he is French, if you get what I mean," Daniel said leaning back in his seat as Tom remembered back in the day when he had a childish crush over the French man, mainly because he thought that the French accent sounded sexy and exotic.

"I have no idea, but you never know, he just might have a surprise up his sleeve for me because he has never missed any one of my fights," Tom said, tapping his fingers against the wheel as he accelerated on the freeway.

The day went well for Tom because he ended up defending his title successfully. It was a celebratory mood for him and his team mates, although they would hold the party at a much later date after their wounds from the fights had healed. When the fight was over, Tom decided to take Daniel for a dinner treat in town before they headed back to the ranch. This was probably going to be their first date since they became an item, and Tom was pretty excited about it all.

"So, what would you like, Mexican or Chinese?" Tom asked as they got into the truck, tossing his bag onto the back seat along with the trophy.

"Hmm, I think I'll go for Mexican, I love their steaks and spices, and Chinese will not really fill up my belly the way that I like it," Daniel said, slamming the door shut and pulling his seat belt over him.

"Well then, Mexicano it is," Tom said putting the truck into gear and pulling out of the parking lot, heading off towards the highway.

He managed to locate a nice romantic up market restaurant on the internet on his cell phone, and then he set his vehicle GPS on to guide him to the address. The delicious aroma of food welcomed them as they entered the dimly lit restaurant that was packed with mainly couples. The head waiter led them to a secluded part of the restaurant with candle lit tables and much more privacy, which was a good thing, because being in love with Danny, Tom was not sure if he would be able to keep his hands to himself. They were handed a menu, and they went ahead to make their orders, which were to be accompanied by bottles of beer.

"This is the first time that I have been to a place that is so classy," Daniel said looking around the room as they waited for their drinks to be brought.

"Yeah, it is a very romantic place, look at the way that those couples are necking over there, while that guy over there clearly has his hands under the woman's dress," Tom said, pointing his chin at some tables not very far from theirs as he slipped one hand under the table and pressed it over Daniel's crotch, making Daniel breath in heavily as his dick twitched in his pants.

"Dude, are you out of your mind, we are in a restaurant and you are going to make me get horny," Daniel said, shifting uncomfortably in his seat as his cock began to harden.

"I'm only doing what everyone else seems to be doing, and besides, this is a romantic bar and restaurant and I don't think that they will really have a problem with it as long as it stays under wraps," Tom said, continuing to tease Danny's dick with his hand, massaging it as it began to get a life of its own.

He pulled his hand away quickly as the waiter returned with the beers, placing a bottle infront of each of them. The waiter went ahead and opened the bottles for them and then left, telling them that their food order would be ready soon. The cold beer felt good going down his throat as Tom took a swig from his bottle, a nice preparation for the great evening that they were about to have. The dinner arrived soon after, and just like Danny had said, it was a very satisfying meal that left them both feeling well filled up. After dinner they began making orders of more beers, and it was not long before they had loosened up and become mellower. Tom moved closer to Danny and began kissing him in the restaurant, no longer caring about who saw them and who did not. The beer made him feel a sudden surge of arousal and if he could, he would have made love to Danny right there and then in the restaurant. The kisses were making him weaker and he felt as if every nerve in his body was alive with erotic desire. His dick became as hard as a rock and it was only his black lover who could make him feel better and relieve him.

"Think maybe we should get moving already, I really can't wait to get home so that I can make love to you like there will be no tomorrow," Tom said, pulling his lips away from Daniel's dark ones and looking at how sexy Daniel looked in the candle light.

"I think that is a perfect idea, any more time spent here and I might end up fucking you right here, and that could turn out quite disastrous," Danny said as Tom raised his hand to call the attention of a waiter so that he could take care of their tab.

"Did you two love birds enjoy your dinner?" the young South American said, looking from Tom to Daniel as if he wished he was one of them, and from the way that he was acting, anyone could tell that he was gay and very lonely.

"Definitely, Tony, the food and everything else was great," Tom said, pulling out his wallet and handing him a couple of twenty dollar bills. "Keep the change, Tony, and see you around some other time."

"Thank you sir," he said looking at Tom and then turning to look at Danny. "You are a very lucky person, honey, take good care of him."

In the car, as soon as Tom put it into gear and set off, Daniel leaned over to the driver's side, his hands going down to Tom's crotch and beginning to unzip his pants. he slipped his hand into the pants and pulled Tom's boxer down over his dick, before taking a hold of the cock and pulling it out of the crotch. Daniel wrapped his fingers around the base of his dick and then lowered his head down to Tom's crotch, beginning to lick the tip of the pecker. Tom could barely concentrate on the road as renewed passion and pleasure flooded into his body. He had become accustomed to Danny sucking him off in the most pleasurable ways, and he had to really focus on the road as Danny ran his tongue over the tip of his cock, spreading the precum deliciously over the sensitive skin of the head. He gripped the wheel tightly, barely breathing as Daniel began taking more and more of his shaft into his mouth, sucking on it as he played his tongue over the skin. Tom had to swerve the car hard to avoid a pothole as the heat within his balls heightened tremendously. This was really crazy, getting his dick blown as he drove through the night with the risk of a traffic cop busting them, and yet he was enjoying it more than anything before.

Danny took his cock all the way into his mouth, and Tom felt the head slipping into Daniel's throat. He had gotten used to it and no longer gagged, instead taking it like a real lover who had sucked on the cock a million and one times. The heat within the love rod had become almost impossible, and Tom groaned out his pleasure. He knew that there was an eminent release that would come very soon, and he had a feeling that it was going to be very explosive. He gripped the steering wheel even tighter as he felt a sudden surge of desire erupting within him. His hot fluid shot through the love rod and out of the eye, flooding into Daniel's mouth. Daniel clamped his lips around the cock, jerking the length furiously with his hand as he sucked in all of Tom's cum. Tom was in heaven as shot after shot of his load filled Daniel's mouth until no more could come out. When he was done coming, Daniel licked his dick dry and then tucked it back into Tom's pants and zipped them up.

CHAPTER 11

Valerie was pacing the living room up and down when Tom and Daniel arrived back at the ranch house. He dashed out of the house as soon as the truck pulled up the driveway, running to Tom's door and pulling it open.

"I'm so glad that you are back, Tom, there has been a terrible accident," he said quickly, and from the tone of his voice, Tom could tell that it was something very serious.

"What is it, Valerie, you are scaring me?" Tom said, getting out of the truck quickly.

"What is happening, Tom, what accident are you talking about?" Daniel also asked, running around the truck.

"It is your dad and your mother," Valerie said hesitantly, and Tom had a feeling that the worst had happened.

"What happened to my parents, Valerie, where are they?" Tom asked, grabbing Valerie by the collars and pulling him close.

"Cool down, Tom, let him tell us what happened," Daniel said, pulling Tom away and holding him tight.

"Mr. and Mrs. Sharpe were in accident and they are in very serious condition, Tom. The hospital just called a few minutes ago and I was just about to call you when you arrived," Valerie said, the news slapping Tom across the face like a cold wind, and his heart feeling as if it was going to stop.

"What?" Tom asked, breath disappearing from his lungs as he collapsed heavily against Daniel.

"Come on, guys, I'll drive us there so that we can find out the actual details of what happened," Daniel said, helping Tom around the truck and putting him in the driver's side of the truck.

CHAPTER 12

Daniel and Valerie both knew just how close Tom and his parents were, and especially being that he had been an only child. Tom seemed to have been hit hard by the news and he sat as if in a daze on the driver's seat, while Valerie sat on the back seat. Daniel drove the truck fast, praying by all means that nothing serious at all had happened to Thomas and Pricilla. They were the parents of his new lover, and the only people who had been so kind to take him in almost as if he were their child, and if anything bad happened, he did not know how he would be able to stand it. He also knew that it would completely seep the strength away from Tom just like it had already done. Daniel had lost his parents and understood just what it felt like to lose someone special to him, and he was praying that the same would not happen to Tom. He was way too fragile to face a loss, and Daniel was not sure if he would ever be able to recover from the loss. An hour and a half later, they pulled up outside the hospital and before Daniel had the time to look for a parking lot, Tom and Valerie had dashed out of the car and into the building. Daniel quickly parked the truck and dashed into the building after Tom and Valerie, but when he got to the reception, they were nowhere to be seen.

"May I help you, young man?" a young Lady at the counter said to him.

"Yes, I'm looking for two accident victims who were brought here probably about two hours ago, a man and a woman, Thomas and Pricilla Langley Sharpe," he said to the receptionist quickly.

"And who are you?" she asked patiently as Daniel cursed under his breath.

"I am like a son to them, they took me in after my parents died," he said, uncomfortable at the way that the young woman seemed to be studying him, almost as if she was undressing him and doing to him things that only Tom could.

"Are you with the other two people who just came in?" she said, leaning forward and showing off her generous cleavage.

"Yes, they left me looking for a parking lot."

"Well, handsome, you can go to the ER down that corridor, and then maybe after that you could come back and leave me your number. I'm sure that you and I-"

Daniel ran off down the corridor not bothering to hear the rest of her response even though he heard her tone of disappointment. He found Tom and Valerie standing outside the door of the ER.

"Any news on what is happening?" Daniel asked as he came to a stop next to them.

"Not yet, the doctor asked us to wait here. They are both in surgery and we will determine what will happen after that," Tom said quietly.

"Would any of you like some coffee?" Valerie asked. "It looks like it is going to be one hell of a long night here."

"Yes, please bring us both some, without any cream," Daniel replied on their behalf, figuring that it would help get rid of the alcohol in their systems.

"I hope that nothing serious has happened to them, I don't know if I'll ever be able to live if something bad happens to them, Danny, they have been so good to me," Tom said with tears on the brim of his eyes.

"We got to keep our hopes up, they are going to pull through this and tomorrow we will be back home, all four of us," Daniel said, hoping that he too could believe his own words.

"You know what I think, Danny, maybe this is some sort of payback, maybe they never really wanted us to be together at all, and the fact that we hitched up when they were away could have led to all of this bad luck," Tom said, thoughtfully.

"Stop being paranoid, Tom, I don't think that it has anything to do with us, and like I said, they are going to be just fine," Daniel said, comfortingly.

Valerie arrived with the coffee moments later, and a nurse told them to go to the waiting room and await any results there, since in the corridor, they were blocking the way. Daniel held Tom's hand leading him to the waiting room and showing him to a seat. It was probably the longest night of their lives, because hours later, the first Ray's of the sun shone into the building as morning arrived.

"Maybe you two should go on back to the ranch, I'll hang around here and keep you informed in case of anything," Valerie said, eyeing the two young men, and especially Tom worriedly.

"I wanna see my mom and dad before I leave this place," Tom said stubbornly.

"I think Valerie is right, you need to get some rest, it has been a hectic weekend and you might end up in one of the wards as a patient if you hang around here much longer," Daniel said, putting his hand around Tom's shoulders and squeezing him, his own heart torn from seeing his lover like this.

"Thank you, Daniel, take him home for some rest, I'll keep you on top of things here," Valerie said, yawning as Tom also yawned.

"Okay, you win, I'm going home, but I'll be back within a couple of hours if I do not hear from you," Tom said, throwing his hands in the air as he stood up. "Let's get out of here, Danny."

They drove home in an awkward silence and when they got home, Danny escorted Tom to his bedroom so that he could rest.

"I guess I'll see you later, huh, get some sleep, honey," Daniel asked, heading back to the door as Tom undressed.

"Don't leave, Danny, I don't wanna be alone, stay with me please," Tom said, getting onto his bed, stark naked as Daniel turned to look at him.

"Okay, Tom, let me just use the bathroom," Daniel said, locking the door and walking back into the bedroom, heading toward the bathroom.

Moments later, he came back out and stripped off his clothes, joining Tom on the bed. The sleep that had accumulated quickly took them over, and the dark body held the white one as both men dozed off soon enough.

CHAPTER 13

Thomas Langley Sharpe II felt pain all over as he struggled to open his eyes. All that he could remember was a truck losing control and coming head on in their lane for a deadly accident. He heard Pricilla screaming, and that was the last thing he could recall. Now he was somewhere, probably in heaven, waiting for God to call him in, although he could hear the beep of machines. He struggled to open his eyes again but all that he could see was a hazy light. He tried to move his hands and legs, but they felt as if they were dead. Panic suddenly overcame him, he had been injured in an accident and was probably on the verge of death.

"Doctor," he heard Valerie's worried voice shouting, "I think that he has just woken up, his eyes are moving."

Moments later there was a scuffling of feet and Thomas heard a female voice asking Valerie to step out of the room. He wondered if he was still alive or if he was already dead. Nothing on his body seemed to be working apart from his ears.

"Thomas, can you hear me?" a male voice asked. "Try and move your eyes if you can hear me."

Thomas could hear the voice well, and he tried to open his eyes again. He also tried to move his lips although they were still very heavy. He felt as if he was heavily sedated, his mind groggy. The sound of his wife screaming as the truck slammed into their car came back to his mind.

"Pricilla," he managed to say softly, barely discernible. "Where is my wife? What happened?"

"Thomas," the male voice said patiently and slowly. "You were involved in an accident."

"Priscilla, where is she, tell her to come and see me," he said with trouble.

"I'm sorry Thomas, but we lost her a few minutes ago. The injuries on her brain were to severe and she could not fight it any longer. We nearly thought that we were going to lose you too," the male voice said, and Thomas felt as if he had just lost his reason to live.

What reason did he have for living if Pricilla was gone? He remembered the day that he had met her while they were in college, and he had proposed to her two weeks later. It had been like some sort of fairytale romance right to the very end, and she had even borne him the best gift of his life, Tom Langley Sharpe III. Tom had been his inspiration throughout, and everything that he had achieved had been for his son. Now for some reason, Thomas felt as if it was his time to leave so that Tom could take over from where he had left off. He closed his eyes once again and darkness filled them. He could see Pricilla somewhere up in the clouds, and she was dressed in white smiling down at him. Had she already made it to heaven, he wanted to ask her.

"Make sure that Tom is happy before you come and join me here," Pricilla said, her voice echoing in his head. "I'll be waiting for you right here, honey, go on back and make sure that our son is happy."

Thomas tried to reply, but his voice could not come out. Instead Pricilla waved at him, and just like she had appeared, she was gone. Thomas tried calling her name to ask her not to leave him, but she never came back, her words still echoing in his mind. If it was her last wish for him to make sure that their son was happy, then he was going to grant her that wish. He was going to make that wish come true before he joined her where she was, and it was going to have to be pretty soon because he felt as if he did not have the strength to keep on fighting for life. Thomas felt the pain seething through his body again, and he struggled to open his eyes when he felt an electric bump on his chest.

"We have him again, doctor, we almost lost him, but we have him," a female voice said as the sound of beeping machines came back into Thomas's life.

"Give him a shot to stabilize him, I don't think we will lose him again," a male voice said quickly amid a shuffle of sounds.

Thomas felt a needle piercing into his bicep and moments later most of the pain that he was feeling began to fade away. He tried to open his eyes, and this time he could make out figures of people in white and blue uniforms moving rapidly around his bed. He was in hospital and it looks like they had just saved his life. He drifted off into an uneasy sleep where he dreamt of his son, Tom. He knew that Tom was gay and very madly in love with Daniel, and Thomas also knew that if there was someone who could take care of Tom very well in his absence, it was going to be Daniel. Maybe that is what Pricilla had meant when she had told him to make sure that Tom was happy before Thomas went to join her wherever she was. She wanted him to give their son his blessings so that he could live his life without any regrets, and although Thomas knew that he might never make it to doing so, he was going to do his best. The good thing about it all, was that he had already indicated it on his will, saying that if Tom was to become an item with Daniel, they could split their wealth after a prenup was signed, although not that he thought that the need to use the prenup would ever come in handy. Daniel was a good young man and never one to go after material things.

CHAPTER 14

"Excuse me sir, but we managed to save Mr. Sharpe and he is now resting, you can go in and see him, but be careful not to wake him up. His condition is very delicate and anything small could make him relapse into a coma," the doctor said to Valerie, who got up from his seat quickly.

"Thank you, doctor," he said, walking towards the corridor that led to the room where Thomas was.

He was still trying to digest the news of Pricilla's death and wondering how he was going to break the news to Tom. It was going to break the young man, but it was a rite of passage in life and everyone had to use that lane at some point in their lives. It was a good thing that Tom had finally realized that he was madly in love with Daniel and let him know about it, since it was pretty evident from the way that they had been acting. He himself was gay and had been right from a tender age, and it was the best thing that could have happened to him. He'd had many lovers in the past but now as he grew older, he preferred to be alone and dedicate himself to working for Thomas and his family, since they were like the family that he never had. As a matter of fact, they were the only family that he knew and that is why Pricilla's death pained him so much and why he could feel the pain that Thomas was going through right now, almost as if he were in his place.

He had wanted to drive Thomas to their business weekend, but Thomas was as stubborn as a mule and had insisted that Valerie spend the weekend off doing something that he liked. Valerie had therefore hang around New Orleans with an old flame of his, indulging in passionate desire. He kind of blamed himself for all that had happened, since had he been the chauffeur, none of this would have happened, and Thomas and Pricilla would be home safe and sound, and Tom would still have his mother alive. He felt tears stinging his eyes as he turned the knob to the room and pushed the door open, stepping into the room and looking at Thomas. The man whom he knew as strong and powerful now lay there in the hospital bed like some piece of discarded cabbage, unable to do a thing. He had drips all over and an oxygen mask across his mouth and nose. Pity threatened to overwhelm Valerie as he pulled up a seat beside the bed and sat on it, putting his hand over Thomas's.

"Please, sir, don't leave us so soon. I know that you are strong enough to pull it through this one, think of Tom and all of the other people who care for you at the ranch, we can't afford to lose you right now," Valerie said with tears in his eyes.

He went ahead to say a little prayer, both for Thomas and for his departed wife. He also prayed that Tom was alright back home, although he knew that Daniel was taking good care of him. If they were to lose both Thomas and Pricilla, it was going to be a huge blow, and especially to Tom. Tom was a very emotional young man when it came to the people that he cared for, and Valerie was not very sure if he would ever get through such a loss. There was also the business aspect of things. Tom was still learning the ropes of running the ranch and there was no better teacher other than his own dad, the man who had brought up the ranch from nothing into one of the most successful ranches in the county. The only other person who knew all of the running of the ranch was Valerie, since he was Thomas Sharpe's right hand man, but he was not really sure if he knew enough to become Tom's teacher. He had been sitting by the side of the bed for what seemed like an eternity, hoping to see an improvement in his boss's condition and was just dozing off when he thought he heard a movement. Looking at Thomas quickly, Valerie was surprised to see his eyes wide open and looking at him.

"Valerie," Thomas said in a feeble voice. "W-w-where i-is T-Tom?"

"Thomas, please try not to talk, relax, the doctor will be here in a minute," Valerie said quickly, beginning to get up from the chair.

"N-no, Valerie, s-sit down, don't call the doctor, I need to talk to you," Valerie could tell the urgency of Thomas's voice despite the fact that he was struggling to talk, and he sat back down in his chair, looking at Thomas, who looked a lot more at peace with himself.

"Where is my son?" he asked, tilting his eyes to look at Valerie.

"They spent the whole night here, and I had to send them off to get some rest almost an hour ago, sir, he was pretty shaken up," the Frenchman said.

"I don't think that I have very much time, but if you have your cell phone with you, I would like for you to record me as I say something to him. his mother has just spoken to me, and I also feel that it is important that I tell him this before I die," Thomas said, his voice a lot more stable now to the point where Valerie thought he was bluffing about the whole death thing.

"You are going to be just fine, sir, and when they discharge you, I'm taking you back to the ranch with me-"

"Listen to me very carefully, Valerie, I don't have very much time, and I would like you to do as I say. I strength is leaving me fast, get your phone out," Thomas insisted, and despite his disapproval, Valerie pulled out his cell phone and put on the video recorder.

Thomas spoke for almost thirty minutes as Valerie recorded him, thinking of it all as one dirty joke since Thomas was going to fight it out and get out of here alive. When Thomas was done, he somehow managed to squeeze Valerie's hand, which was still on his.

"Thank you Valerie, please take good care of my son and Daniel for me, and make sure that they are happy. I have to go now, I don't have any more strength left in me, goodbye my dearest friend," he said, and with that, his grip loosened and then there was the incessant beeping of machines.

Nurses and doctors came running into the room, and tears filled Valerie's eyes as he sobbed openly, the doctor announcing Thomas dead. A sense of deep loss overwhelmed him, but at least his two bosses were now in a better place.

Valerie watched as they took the body to the morgue, all of his strength suddenly gone. Some of the most important people in his life had just passed away and he was left with the heaviest duty of breaking the news to Tom. After talking to funeral organizers, Valerie pulled out his cell phone number and dialed Tom's number. It was now time to break the dreadful news, the earlier, the better.

CHAPTER 15

Tom groaned as he felt the thickness of Daniel's cock pressing into his butt hole. "Oh fuck, put some more lube on it, there is too much friction," he said to Daniel, pulling away from his dark lover.

"Right up, honey," Daniel said, reaching for the tube of KY and spreading some of the jelly generously over his dick and some over the rim of the butt hole.

Tom was on his hands and knees on his bed, naked to the bone, and his head was down on the mattress with his ass in the air behind him. Daniel was standing at the back of the bed directly behind Tom with his feet on the ground. Tom relaxed a little when he felt the coldness of the lube being rubbed over his butt crack he closed his eyes when he felt Daniel parting his butt cheeks again, and moments later, he felt the tip of his dick pushing into his butt hole.

"Oh yeah, that feels good, Danny, make love to me, make love to me like I belong to you," Tom said, his own cock hard with arousal.

As Daniel began pushing his dick into Tom's butt hole slowly, he reached around Tom and took a hold of his dick, wrapping his fingers around the thickness. Tom groaned once again as Daniel began jerking his dick pleasurably with his still lubed hand. As he jerked Tom's cock, Daniel pressed his own dick deeper and deeper into Tom's butt, filling him up the way that he loved to be filled up. Tom had a feeling that this was going to be the most intense love making that they had ever had, and it had even made him forget about his parents temporarily as arousal and desire consumed him alive. Daniel pushed his dark thickness into Tom's white tightness, stopping every few inches to let Tom's butt hole become adjusted to the intruding thickness.

When the black monster cock was fully inserted inside Tom's ass hole, Daniel began fucking him hard and fast, driving his dick in and out of Tom's ass in long delicious strokes. He pushed the cock in until it completely disappeared into the

Jodie Sloan

butt hole, before pulling out until just the tip was inserted. As he fucked him from behind, Danny jerked Tom's cock in the same long strokes, and Tom felt as if he had died and gone to heaven. The pleasure was so intense, and coupled with the fact that he was madly in love with his dark skinned prince, he was totally enjoying it. The thickness of the dark shaft was rubbing pleasurably over Tom's hymen, and Tom could not help but moan. Each stroke became harder and faster as did the movement of the hand over his dick, and Tom felt the heat within him beginning to rise to uncontrollable levels.

His balls were on fire and he could feel the first signs of his climax beginning to build. He began moving his butt back to meet the pounding cock, and it was not long before he felt Daniel's cock stiffening within his butt hole. Tom felt hot jets of jism shooting into his butt hole, the heat giving him a good feeling that made it impossible for him to hold back his own orgasm. The heat of his climax soared through his love rod erupting onto Danny's fingers and shooting onto the bed. As semen filled his ass hole, his semen splashed onto the bed, and when both men were done coming, they collapsed onto the bed, lying on Tom's cum and not giving a care in the world.

CHAPTER 16

It was a long and leisurely dip in the bath tub, and Daniel was seated opposite Tom, looking at him as they enjoyed the feel of the warm water against their skin. They had made love quite a lot and right now all that they wanted was a nice dip in the tub before heading downstairs for some food to get back the calories that they had used up, and then head back into town to see how their parents were doing at the hospital. Daniel considered Thomas and Pricilla as his parents too, and Thomas had even asked him to call him dad, and that is exactly what Daniel did. He had a strange feeling inside him, almost as if there was something wrong, but he could not quite understand it, and so he kept it to himself. His intuition was never wrong, and he had a feeling that something awful had happened at the hospital. It was the same sort of feeling like the one that he had felt the day that his parents had died. He had been a very young boy back then, but he had never been able to forget how he felt, the intuition.

"I think we had better get dressed and get back into the city to check on the folks," he said to Tom, who was leaning back in the tub with his eyes closed.

"Think they are going to be okay?" Tom slowly opened his eyes.

"I don't know, I have this strange feeling, and it is making me sort of uncomfortable, how comes Valerie has not called us until now, don't you think it is strange?" Daniel said, stepping out of the bathtub and reaching for a towel to begin drying himself.

"If anything bad had happened, I'm sure that he would have called us already," Tom said, and Daniel could feel his eyes hovering over his cock as Tom studied him.

"Whatever, stop staring at me like that, if you make me horny I might have to make love to you once again, come on, we had better get moving," Danny said, his intuition becoming even stronger, something had definitely happened, and it was not good, he could feel it all through himself.

Just then the phone in Tom's bedroom went off, and Daniel now had the worst feeling, his fears were just about to be confirmed. When he looked at Tom, he had turned as white as a sheet as he made his way out of the water like a robot and reached for a towel.

"I'll get it," Daniel said, "you dry yourself."

Daniel tied the towel around his waist and made his way out of the bathroom and into the bedroom, dashing to the phone and picking up the receiver.

"Hello?" he said in almost a whisper.

"Hi Daniel?" Valerie said into the phone.

"Valerie, finally, is everything all right, how are the old folks doing?" Daniel asked quickly, his curiosity killing him, although from the tension in Valerie's voice, he had a feeling that his intuition was right.

"Danny, I'm afraid that I have some bad news for you guys," Valerie said, and Daniel could tell that he was buying time, trying to find the right words. "Where is Tom?"

"He is in the bathroom, what is it, Valerie?" Daniel asked.

"Wait for me at the ranch house, I have some news for you and a message from Mr. Thomas. I'll be there in less than an hour," he said, hanging up before Daniel could say another word and leaving him more confused than ever.

"Who was that, and what did they want? Is there any news from the hospital?" Tom asked, walking out of the bathroom quickly.

"It was Valerie, and he sounded very strange indeed," Daniel said, trying to make out their conversation.

"What did he say, how are mom and dad doing, any news?" Tom asked impatiently.

"Well, he said that he has bad news and also that he has a message for us from dad. He said that he will be here in less than an hour, and that we should wait for him for him here," Daniel recalled what he had just been told.

"What does that mean, is he coming with them?" Tom was full of questions. "Maybe they are injured but alive or else how would he get a message from dad, and what the hell could the message be?"

"I'm just as confused as you are, Tom, come on, get dressed, I'll meet you down in the kitchen shortly," Daniel said, tightening the towel around his waist as he made his way out of Tom's bedroom and headed off to his own to get changed into fresh clothes.

Ten minutes later, Danny was seated on one of the bar stools in the kitchen whacking down a double beef and cheese burger when Tom came and joined him. They ate in silence, each of them wondering what Valerie had to say as they waited for him impatiently. Anita pulled on a sad and worried face and sauntered out of the kitchen. Something was definitely amiss here, and it looked like even Anita knew it too. Tom and Daniel both jumped when they heard a car pull into the driveway, and they quickly dashed out to see who it was. Valerie came out of a cab looking exhausted and much older than he was. Just looking at him was enough to bring tears to Daniel's eyes, and he had to fight them back and act brave for Tom's sake. Valerie paid the cabbie and then came up the porch, his shoulders slouched forward.

"Talk to us, Valerie, how did it go at the hospital, how are mom and dad doing?" Tom demanded, and Daniel could tell the answer to the questions by just looking at Valerie.

"Calm down my boy, let us go inside and talk from there, and besides, I'm starving although I don't really have an appetite," Valerie said, walking past Tom and Daniel as if he did not want them to read his mind.

Daniel knew that the worst had happened, he could feel it even without words. When he looked over at Tom, he could see tears on the brim of his eyes. Tom too had sensed it but was just waiting to hear it from the horse's mouth in order for him to believe it. Daniel's intuition continued haunting him, this was more than just death, something horrible was going to happen, although he could not quite figure out what it was, and it was going to involve Tom. He walked quickly behind Tom, eager to prevent him from doing anything stupid when the news was finally broken to them. The bad feeling would not leave him, and he could even taste the bitter taste of bile in his throat. Valerie went into the kitchen, where as if knowing what was happening, Anita had a mug of coffee and a burger waiting for him.

"Welcome back home, Valerie," she smiled at him, setting the coffee and the burger before him. "You should eat before you do anything else."

"Thank you, Valerie, that is exactly what I was telling the boys here, I'm famished," Valerie said, sipping on his coffee.

CHAPTER 17

Tom had a feeling that something had gone terribly wrong somewhere, but he could not imagine what it was. Surely, the worst that could have happened to his parents would be getting injured and nothing more. The mystery that was shrouding Valerie's odd behavior made him even more curious, but he decided to wait patiently until the Frenchman finished his food. He had to be hungry and tired having spent most of the night and morning at the hospital, and it was only fair. Tom wondered what message his dad had for them. Whatever it was, he would wait to hear it directly from his dad, in the meantime, all that he wanted to know was how they were doing at the hospital. Guilt suddenly hit him like a slap on the cheek. While his parents were hurting in hospital, he had been busy having a good time making love with Danny. If anything happened to them, he would never forgive himself for that.

"Well, Valerie, before we go any further, can you tell me just how the old man and old Lady are doing in the hospital, I'll listen to whatever dad had to say after I determine just how they are," Tom said as soon as Valerie had finished eating up his brunch.

"It has been a very tough morning for me at the hospital, Tom, and I'm afraid that I have some very bad news. Mr. Thomas and Mrs. Pricilla passed away this morning. Your mother passed away while undergoing surgery, while your dad passed away later. We even got time to talk, and he left me a message for you," Valerie said slowly, taking his time before looking up at both Tom and Daniel.

"What, Valerie, are you sure about what you are saying?" Tom asked as Daniel rushed by his side to hold him. "Move away from me, Danny, I think that you might be the reason why all of this happened."

"Tom-" Daniel began, but Tom had become wild and he interrupted him harshly.

"Shut up, Daniel, being with you must be the reason why my dad lost control of the car. It was a bit mistake because they expected you to be my brother, not my lover. I'll never forgive you nor myself for this," Tom fumed, smashing a mug against the wall.

"Tom, I think that you had better listen to what your dad had to say before you come to any conclusions that you might regret," Valerie tried to intervene, pulling his smart phone out of his pocket.

"Shut up, Valerie, you are probably the one who told my parents that I'm gay, I hate all of you. Just get out of my sight, will you," Tom shouted at the top of his voice.

CHAPTER 18

The words that Tom was saying were the most hurtful words that Daniel had ever heard, blaming the death of his parents on their relationship. Daniel swallowed hard, a knot forming in his throat.

"Tom, maybe you should chill out a little, the shock is what has got you like this," Daniel said, trying to move closer to Tom, although Tom clearly did not want anyone around him, because he raised his hand into the air as if to stop him.

"Danny, I said please leave me alone," he said, and Daniel's heart blade for the pain the love of his life was feeling.

He too was affected by the loss of two people who had become key pillars in his life but he had to control himself for the sake of his friend. Tears stung his eyes and began flowing down his cheeks as Valerie came over to him and put an arm around his shoulder.

"It is okay, my son, come with me, let us give him some time to mourn his mother and father. He will be alright once the initial shock wears off and the reality checks in. it is only normal for him to behave this way," Valerie said, leading him out of the kitchen and to the living room.

"Why, Valerie, why did they have to die, they were such good people?" Daniel said as the reality of the matter hit home and he began crying without holding back.

"Everything goes with gods time, my son, he is the one who chooses for us what time we must leave this world, and we have to learn how to accept it," Valerie said soothingly, although Daniel could sense the feeling of loss that he also felt.

"UUiii, somebody HELP, Master Tom has fainted," Anita screamed, her voice echoing throughout the house just as Valerie and Daniel were getting seated.

They immediately jumped up and dashed back to the kitchen. Tom had collapsed onto the floor, and Daniel immediately rushed over to him and crouched next to him, taking his wrist to get a feel of his pulse.

"He is still alive, Valerie, call 911, we need an ambulance immediately," he shouted, gathering his lover into his arms as new tears poured from his eyes freely.

He could not afford to lose his new found love too, and if he did, he would probably follow him to his grave. He crossed his fingers, saying a silent prayer as they waited for the paramedics to arrive. It seemed like an eternity before the paramedics finally arrived and carried Tom out to the ambulance. Daniel never left his side for a second and even rode in the ambulance with him. On arrival, Tom was rushed into the emergency room where Daniel was not allowed to enter. For the first time, Daniel thought about God and prayed over and over for Tom as the doctors checked him out.

SECOND CHANCE

CHAPTER 19

It had been exactly two months since Thomas Langley Sharpe II and Pricilla had died, and although things for Tom had been hard, he was slowly coming to terms with it. Valerie had shown him pretty much how everything was run around the ranch, and he had even begun turning profits. And then there was Daniel. At first he had blamed his parent's death on his gay relationship with Daniel. Valerie had convinced him to listen to the recording that his father had left for him before he died, telling him that he wanted Daniel and Tom to be happy together. They had therefore become an item again, and their love was now blossoming more than ever.

"I'm still really considering participating in the horse races, Eagle has become really fast, and I think that chances of winning or being among the leaders are very high, Tom said, staring into the air as he lazed in bed with Daniel. Eagle happened to be a race horse that Tom's dad had bought for him before he passed away.

"If your heart is into racing, then I don't see why you should not give it a chance," Daniel said, getting out of bed and making his way towards the bathroom, his naked body looking sexier than ever.

Tom watched his lover walking to the bathroom, his muscles tense and his chocolate colored cock looking even more delicious than ever. Despite the fact that they had made love at night, Tom found himself starting to get aroused, looking at Daniel and remembering of the sweetness that he had given him at night. Daniel was truly a blessing in his life, and he did not know how he would ever be able to appreciate him enough in his life. Daniel walked out of the bathroom moments later, and Tom's eyes went to his chocolate colored cock. It was semi erect and the only thing that Tom could think of was sucking it to life and then doing naughty things with it. He felt his own dick rising to life, becoming hard with arousal, as his balls tightened, the heat within them burning with desire.

"If you are going to play with the top jockeys, you are going to have to put in quite some practice...." Danny stopped when he saw the way that Tom was staring at his dick as if he was seeing it for the first time. "Why are you staring at my cock like that?"

"I don't know, but everytime that I see it, I tend to get turned on more and imagine myself doing dirty delicious things with it. Right now I'm thinking of giving you a good blowjob and then taking you deep inside my ass, how does that sound?" Tom said, watching the dark cock beginning to harden as he imagined it inside his white ass, pounding him pleasurably.

"I think the cock can speak on my behalf," Danny said, wrapping his fingers around the girth of his now already rock hard dick and beginning to jerk it up and down as he made his way to the bed slowly, his eyes never leaving Tom's.

Tom's heart skipped when he felt the weight of Danny's weight on the bed, and as he sat up on his elbow, Danny moved next to him, putting his free hand around Tom's neck and pulling him towards him. Dark lips fused over white lips as the two men began kissing hungrily, their tongues playing erotically over each other. Tom felt his cock becoming even harder than ever, as an intense arousal overcame him. He reached his hand down to Daniel's cock and wrapped his fingers around it, beginning to jerk it slowly as he played his thumb over the tip and spreading the precum which had quickly pooled on the slip at the tip over the sensitive skin of the head. Daniel did the same, his dark fingers encompassing Tom's white cock as he too began to jerk it, heightening the arousal that both men were feeling. Tom felt his need pulsating with the need to pleasure and be pleasured sexually.

"I want your cock in my mouth," he said urgently, his voice hoarse with arousal.

"And I want yours too, how about we do a 69 if it can be called that," Daniel said, his voice equally loaded with desire.

Tom pushed Daniel onto his back and then got on top of him, straddling his face with his balls directly above Daniel's head. Tom leaned forward, reaching for Daniel's dick and wrapping his fingers around the base of the ebony cock. Moving his face down, he wrapped his lips around the thick delicious head, beginning to suck on it. Daniel also took a hold of Tom's dick and adjusted it so that he could take it into his mouth, and Tom groaned over Daniel's dick when he felt Daniel beginning to suck on the head of the cock. Tom took the cock deeper and deeper into his mouth, loving way that the thickness stretched his jaws uncomfortably. He could feel Daniel's hot breath tickling his own cock as Daniel moaned onto it. Tom took more and more of the dark cock into his mouth, jerking the base as more and more of the male meat disappeared into his mouth. He felt the huge head pushing into his throat, and Tom just kept pressing on, beginning to deep throat the dick until he felt Danny pulling his mouth off his shaft and then pushing him off.

"I'm going to come in your mouth if you continue blowing my dick like that," Danny said as Tom rolled over.

"And what makes you think that I would not enjoy that, I love the way that your semen tastes, and besides, semen is good for the skin, it slows down the aging process," Tom said as he took a hold of Daniel, making him to get onto his hands and knees.

Tom moved behind Daniel and leaned down, parting his butt cheeks to look at his dark puckered hole. He then lowered his face into the butt crack and sniffed in the butt hole, the delicious male scent sending erotic massages to his dick. Sticking out his tongue, he ran it up and down the butt crack before letting it settle on the rim of the butt hole. He eased his tongue into the butt hole, playing it around and lubricating the butt hole as he pushed it even deeper into the butt hole. Daniel wiggled his butt from side to side, and Tom could tell that he was already dying to have his white cock inserted deep within his ass hole. His own arousal was killing him, and so Tom spat over the butt hole before he got onto his knees behind Daniel. Parting his butt cheeks as wide as possible, Tom took a hold of his cock with his other hand and guided it into Daniel's butt hole, easing the head in slowly and pushing until the pecker was fully inserted within. Tom then reached around Daniel's waist and took a hold of his dick, wrapping his fingers around his dick and beginning to jerk it as he began pounding his dick in and out of Danny's ass.

"Oh fuck, you are so tight, I always feel as if you are a virgin everytime I fuck you," Tom said as he began fucking Daniel faster and harder, his white cock sliding in and out of Daniel's dark butt hole.

Daniel began moaning as Tom moved his dick harder and faster, each stroke more delicious that the previous one. Tom's balls slapped against Daniel's whenever he slammed his dick in, and that only seemed to heighten the pleasure. He closed his eyes, his world filled with the pleasure that he had come to love so much. The heat within his balls heightened, and he knew that he was not very far off from coming. One of his hands was still jerking away at Daniel's cock while the other one held Daniel's hip. The smell of male sex soon filled the room, Tom's crotch slapping against Daniel's buttocks. Daniel's butt hole felt so tight and delicious, it was not long before Tom groaned, pushing his dick deep into the dark butt as he jumped over the edge. His seed went shooting into Daniel's ass, but Daniel pulled away quickly and turned around, his lips closing around Tom's cock as he swallowed the remaining jism. Tom was faint with desire by the time that his climax came to an end, and he dropped onto his hands and knees, wanting to feel Daniel inside him.

Daniel wasted no time moving behind him and parting his butt cheeks. He smeared some of Tom's jism over his ass hole, and then Tom felt the huge dark cock pushing into his butt hole, the thickness rubbing over his hymen sweetly. As Daniel began driving his dick in and out of Tom's butt, Tom moved his butt backwards to meet him, each movement becoming faster and harder. The love rod felt hard and stiff in Tom's butt, just the way that he loved it. Daniel slapped Tom's butt cheek, and Tom groaned when he felt Daniel's hot seed pumping into his butt hole.

CHAPTER 20

Riding alongside Tom and Valerie was quite exciting, and they were on the tracks of the ranch preparing for an upcoming horse race event. Tom had been putting pressure on him to also join the upcoming races, but Daniel was not so sure about that since he felt that he was more of a horse trainer other than a jockey. He had however decided that he was going to do it, just so that he could make Tom happy because Tom believed in him. Tom had been the best thing that had happened to him in his life, and Daniel was willing to do anything for him. He leaned forward, chasing after Valerie and Tom, his black Arabian stallion that he had gotten as a gift from Thomas Langley Sharpe before he died doing her best to keep up with Tom's white stallion and Valerie's mare. Tom was definitely the best of them all, because he easily won the race for the umpteenth time.

"That was quite a race," Valerie said to Tom as they got off their horses. "You are getting better by the day and I think that you will make it at the races."

"And that is the same thing that I keep telling him," Daniel said, swinging off his horse and going over to Tom to give him a warm hug. "I think that you are the best person for this race, Tom, I'm no good."

"You have got to believe in yourself, Danny, focus and believe in yourself, and the attitude will rub onto your horse. That is the only way that one can win or become among the top racers," Tom said, looking into his eyes lovingly.

"I think Tom is right, my boy, you have got to put your mind in a winning frame," Valerie said, and at times Daniel had this feeling that Valerie hoped to be in his shoes as Tom's lover from the way that he looked at them. "Come on, boys, are we still going into New Orleans for dinner, there is this nice place that I used to go dancing when I was still a young lad, I wonder if it is still open?"

"Valerie, surely, you wouldn't wanna come dancing with us, our type of music is completely different from yours," Tom kidded the jovial Frenchman. "and you would get pretty bored since you would have no partner."

"Are you trying to say that I'm that old, and who told you that old men like me cannot have lover's, there are plenty of people out there who would be interested in a lonely French man like me," Valerie joked as they made their way to the mansion.

They freshened up and then met downstairs in the foyer. Daniel was dressed in a cowboy outfit, right from his Stetson down to his studded boots. He was in a tight fitting suede shirt and jeans, the ultimate look. Tom was dressed in a sexy tight fitting shirt that showed off his muscles in a nice way, the sort of way that made Daniel feel like ripping his clothes off and doing dangerously delicious things. He was also dressed in a pair of tight fitting khaki pants, and Daniel could not help but stare at his ass as they walked out of the house. This was one sight that he would never tire of. With a tinge of jealousy, Daniel noted the way that Valerie also had his eyes on Tom's buttocks. At times he wondered if Valerie was gay because he had never seen him showing an interest in women, but neither he nor Tom had the answer to that. Maybe they would find out someday when Valerie felt comfortable enough to tell them.

CHAPTER 21

Valerie was very proud of the two young lovers, and especially Tom who had picked up the broken pieces and moved on swiftly after the death of his parents. He was now an even better manager of the ranch that his father had been and was turning better profits than the ranch had ever made. There was something that he now wanted both of them to know, and that was the reason that he had invited them out to dinner. They had both matured into adults and Valerie felt that it was time that he let them in on something that he had never told anyone close to him. He wanted them to know that he was just like them, gay, since being the younger generation, they seemed to understand it better. Back in his native France, it was never an issue since the French were some of the most open minded people when it came to sex issues.

"Well, gentlemen, here we are," he said, stopping the car outside a gay club that he had stumbled on some time ago.

"From your excitement, I can tell that we are going to have a really good time," Tom said as they got out of the car.

"I'm pretty sure that you two are going to love this place, it is a place discovered by accident some time ago, and the ambience and décor is excellent. I am also pretty sure that you are going to love the sort of clientele that come here," Valerie said, leading the way to the elevators of the building.

CHAPTER 22

Tom wondered what Valerie was up to, although he knew that if he asked him, Valerie could never tell him what was cooking on his mind. The best thing was just to go along with him and wait for the surprise. Tom had never heard of the restaurant where they were going, although judging from the commotion that had been downstairs, it was probably one very popular restaurant and club. The elevator car finally got to their location, and the doors slid open, opening into a room with booming music and many people. At first, Tom did not realize what seemed odd at the joint, and then he realized what felt off. There were many men and women in the club, but each gender was on its own. The women were in couples, just like were the men, a gay club.

"Wait a minute, this place is not what I think it is, is it?" Tom said walking into the room and looking around. "Who would have guessed that such a joint existed in New Orleans?"

"What are you talking about?" Danny asked, looking confused as they followed Valerie to the back of the room.

"Open your eyes, honey, I think this is a gay club, check it out, there are only male couples and female couples here, isn't that awesome," Tom was over the moon.

"That is right, I thought that you deserved to know this place, I usually come by here to pass time when I'm bored, and it is the excellent place to get good company," Valerie said as a guy woke up from the table they were headed to, smiling broadly at Valerie.

"Wait a minute, are you.." Tom began.

"Yes, that is right, I'm gay, and I've been gay ever since. I just never thought it appropriate to let everyone at the ranch know, but your dad, Mr. Thomas, knew about it," Valerie said as the guy who had woken up as they approached walked over to Valerie and sealed his lips onto his, kissing him passionately, and it was evident the way that Valerie reacted to the kiss, a bulge quickly forming inside his pants.

Watching the passionate encounter, Tom found himself beginning to get turned on, his own body reacting heatedly, and he looked over at Danny and blushed. He could see his own desire reflected in Danny's eyes, and he immediately felt his cock hardening with arousal. Somewhere in the recess of the dimly lit room, he could see a man pounding another guy. Both men had their pants down to their ankles, and one of them was bent over yet another man who was seated, sucking on his cock. The other standing man was behind the bent guy, and he had his dick buried deep within his ass hole, drilling it in and out. Tom had never seen anything like this, and he felt arousal coursing through his body. He had heard that there were sex clubs, but he had never imagined that they actually existed, and in New Orleans.

As he and Danny were still standing there, trying to absorb the new experience, they saw Valerie sliding his hand into the pants of the man he was kissing, and through the movement of the material of his pants, they could saw him beginning to jerk on the pecker, rubbing it up and down. Tom had never felt so aroused, since he had never imagined how it would feel watching other people making out. somewhere not too far off were two lesbians also in the process of making out, and one was seated on a chair, her legs parted wide, while another one crouched before her, her face buried in the other ones crotch, eating out her pussy. Hunger for excitement overwhelmed him, and he felt Danny's hand around his waist, steering him towards the counter.

"Fancy for a drink as we prepare ourselves for some erotic action?" he said.

"A really stiff drink will do me a lot of good. Who would have known that Valerie knew of such a place," Tom said, settling onto a bar stool next to Danny.

"What can I get for you, handsome fellas?" the barman, a guy dressed up in a lot of makeup and no clothing on except for a male thong that showed off a long thin cock that was soft.

"Give me something really strong, honey," Tom said, shifting uncomfortably at the way that the barman seemed to be undressing him with his eyes.

"Me too," Danny said.

"You two must be new here. You don't have to be tense, just relax and enjoy yourselves like everybody else. If you would like special services, we offer those too, and I can take you upstairs to choose from a couple of suitors, at a fee of course," he said, sauntering away and coming back with two tumblers, which he began filling with tequila.

Danny arched up his eyebrows with curiosity. "Special services, what exactly do you mean by that?"

"You guys are definitely new here, why don't you two drink up and then I'll explain everything to you," he said, pushing the tumblers towards them.

Tom took his and drained it immediately, closing his eyes as he felt it going through his body, leaving a burning trail behind it, the burning trail reflecting what he was feeling in his crotch. Tom felt his cock hardening even more, and all that he could think of was having it deep in someone's ass, drilling him like it was the end of the world, and that person was Danny.

"Perfect, I can see that you were both in need of a very stiff drink," the barman said, interrupting Tom's thoughts. The barman signaled to one of the waiters, who was also dressed in just a male thong. "Luke here will show you the variety of special services."

They introduced themselves to Luke, who then went ahead to tell them that since it was their first time at the joint, the first drinks were on the house. Asking them to follow him, he led them away from the bar, and as they passed by Valerie, he was on his knees sucking on the other man's cock, and taking it very deep into his mouth, deeper than Tom had ever imagined anyone could take. He almost could not believe that it was Valerie, and everything seemed as if he were in some sort of fairy tale. They followed Luke into a corridor and he led them to the first room, which happened to be a bondage room.

"Everyone has their own fetishes and it is up to you to choose what you want," Luke said as they entered the room. "This place is for the BDSM element and you are free to play with these gentlemen if you wish."

Tom and Daniel looked around in astonishment. There was a man who had his hands and legs bound in a way that the hands and the legs were both wide apart. He was suspended in the air, and there was a man standing behind him with a whip, fucking him as he whipped him across the back. The strapped up man seemed to be both enjoying the pain and the pleasure, and Tom wondered how he did that. Infront of him was another man who was bending forward, and he was busy sucking on the man's cock, laving the length as it moved in and out of his mouth.

"In here there is intense sex that might involve a little pain inflicting, and you are free to choose the role that you wish to play," Luke said, and when Tom looked over at him, he saw his dick hardening in the male thong, a long slender rod whose tip poked out of the waist of the thong.

"Wow, what an outfit you have in here, what else do you have?" Danny asked, his own cock also as hard as a rock.

"Follow me, the next room is for gangbangs," Luke said, leading them to yet another room where there was a lot of hardcore wild sex going on.

There had to be at least ten people making out there, fucking butt, sucking cock, licking butt and so many other erotic things, and the whole room smelled of sex. Tom had always thought that this sort of thing was only found on porn sites on the internet and he almost couldn't believe that he was actually witnessing it live. Despite the images getting him all turned on and horny, Tom could not help but wonder how someone could take on so many people at the same time. He could not even begin to imagine himself having sex with another man other than Danny, it just didn't make sense to him. Maybe it was because he was in love and that was the only thing that mattered. The one thing that he would not mind was making out with his lover infront of other people. It would actually get him really turned on in a delicious way, just the same way that thinking about it had made him.

"I think that I would just rather… you know…" Tom began.

"Fuck?" Luke finished for him.

"Yes, with Danny here. I can't imagine myself with another man, but thanks anyways," Tom finished.

"Yeah, me too, I just can't imagine doing it with someone else," Danny said curtly.

"What a pity, you guys don't know what you are missing out on," Luke said pitifully. "I was hoping to have a little fun with both of you."

"Well, Luke, that is too bad, but you are welcome to watch if you are interested," Danny echoed Tom's thoughts aloud.

"In that case, I don't think that you'll really want to see the rest of the services that we offer," Luke said, strolling out of the room. "Let me take you back to the sex bar, there you are free to do what you want."

Tom and Danny followed him back to the bar, and as they passed by Valerie, he was leaning over a table while behind him his lover had his dick buried deep in his butt. Tom felt arousal coursing through his body in a delicious way. They located an empty table that had cushioned couches somewhere in the room, and Tom sat down next to Danny. Their heads immediately went together, their lips locking over each other as they began kissing passionately. Tom's light skinned lips parted readily as Danny's tongue pushed into his mouth and began probing him, tasting him and getting him even more aroused than ever. Tom felt his blood rushing through his blood as his heart beat even faster, and somewhere from the corner of his eye, he could see Luke looking on enviously. Without pulling his lips away from Danny's, Tom reached his hand down to Danny's crotch and pulled the zipper of his pants open. The only one thing that he wanted right now was the chocolate cock that was hidden in the pants.

Tom pulled the pants open and then slipped his hand into them, pulling the boxers down over the erect cock. He then wrapped his fingers around the pecker and started jerking it up and down. The slimy precum had already pooled over the tip of the cock, and Tom spread it with his thumb over Danny's sensitive cock head, making him groan into his mouth. The dark cock was harder than Tom could ever remember, and now what he wanted to do the most was to get a taste of the delicious precum that he had come to love so much. Driving his tongue deep into Danny's mouth one last time, Tom pulled his lips away from Danny's. He then moved back on the couch and leaned forward, his head going down to Danny's crotch. Wrapping his lips around the tip of the cock, he began sucking on it as he played his tongue over the eye at the tip of the manhood to get a taste of the precum. Tom then began taking more and more of the cock into his mouth, his head moving up and down over the manhood as more and more of the male organ disappeared into his mouth. It was thick and hard, filling up every inch of his mouth as he laved the delicious flesh. He tried to take it as deep as he had seen Valerie taking the other cock into his mouth, although it was almost impossible given the size of the monster cock. He finally felt the thick head slipping past his epiglottis and into his throat, and that was as far as Tom could take it. His own dick was aching with need, and he needed Danny to give it some attention.

Danny seemed to know just what to do, because as soon as Tom pulled his mouth off his shaft, he stood up and pulled his pants off. Tom watched with pride as many of the eyes in the sex club shot to his lover's crotch, looking at the erect black snake with envy. That was a moment that Tom would never forget, and he immediately wanted Danny inside him, not in his mouth, but in his anus. He also got up and pulled his pants down, removing a bottle of KY lube from his pocket and handing it to Danny. Tom then got onto his knees on the couch and leaned forward, resting his hands on the back rest. Danny pulled the cap of the lube open and then parting Danny's butt cheeks, squeezed some of the cold jelly into his butt crack. Danny then went ahead to spread the lube over the butt hole as well as squeeze some onto his dick. Tom closed his eyes, his whole body more alert than ever as he felt Danny's thickness pushing into his butt hole. He heard sighs from the onlookers as more and more of the dark meat penetrated her butt hole, slowly by slowly as the butt hole adjusted to the new size within it.

The cock was soon fully inserted in Tom's ass hole, and Danny reached one hand around Tom's waist and took a hold of his dick, beginning to jerk it as he pumped his dick in and out of Tom's butt. Tom could not remember when he had ever felt so much desire before, maybe due to the fact that there were people actually watching them have sex. They were sharing one of their most intimate moments with an audience, and that was by far the cream of the love making. His balls were boiling with desire, and the heat in his love rod was increasing by the second as Danny jerked it. Tom loved the way that Danny's cock rubbed over his hymen, and the pleasure was making his own orgasm bubble to the surface. Suddenly, Tom felt Danny's cock stiffening within his butt.

"Urgh, I'm coming," Danny grunted, just as the first jet of jism shot into Tom's butt hole.

The intensity of the climax was so intense, Tom felt his own climax exploding, his semen shooting into the air. Before he knew what was happening, Luke had fused his lips over the head of his cock, and he sucked out every last drop of his seed, swallowing it. Never in his entire being had love making felt so intense before.

CHAPTER 23

It had been a couple of days since they went to the club, and Danny was feeling more erotically refreshed than ever. Having sex infront of everyone had sort of added spice to their relationship, and now more than ever, Danny was more in love with Tom.

"I think that it is going to be fun at the tracks today, I have a hunch that you are going to e among the top jockeys," Tom said, walking into the room and startling Danny out of his thoughts.

"I really don't know about all this, I have a sort of bad feeling about this whole thing, maybe you should race alone," Danny said, opening up how he really felt, because there was a sixth sense telling him not to participate in the derby.

"Oh, come on, honey, I think that you are just getting butterflies, everything is going to go just fine. We have some of the best horses in the country, and we too are some of the best jockeys too. believe me, we are going to do just fine, and besides, look at all of the money that is involved in the races, it is in the millions," Tom said, walking into the wardrobe and pulling out his riding gear to inspect it.

"Well, if you say so, but I'm only doing this because I love you, or else I would never have gone ahead with such a crazy idea," Danny said, moving behind Tom and wrapping his hands around his waist. "I am so crazy in love, I am willing to do the craziest of things for you."

"And I promise to love you back just the same way that you love me, I too am willing to do anything for you, and I would die if anything were to happen to you," Tom said, turning around and kissing Danny lightly on the lips. "Come on, the truck outside is waiting, and we don't wanna be late."

Grabbing their things they made their way out of the room. Danny still had a bad feeling about the whole racing issue, and he felt as if he was not ready for it. The truck with the horse carriage was ready to leave, and Valerie was busy double checking to see if everything was alright.

"Ready to go boys, I nearly thought that you had changed your mind about going to the derby," Valerie smiled at them as they approached him. "The horses are set and I think that we are going to do very well since the practice has been intense over the past few days."

"Yeah, I'm in a winning mood today, and I think that our team is going to outdo itself, we are born champions," Tom smiled broadly, sliding onto the back seat of the truck.

Danny was exceptionally quiet as they rode to the racecourse in New Orleans. He was feeling sort of tense within and had a premonition of something bad happening, although he could not quite place his finger on what it was. He sat on the passenger seat beside Valerie, who was at the wheel and was humming away at some Elvis Presley ballad. Tom too was extremely quiet, but Danny had the feeling that he could smell his success. When they got to the racecourse, there was a buzz of activity going on there, and there were many other people and animals there. Bets were being made by racing enthusiasts, and the first thing that Valerie did was to go ahead and place a huge bet running into millions on Eagle, Tom's horse. Danny was also a jockey, but he too placed a bet on Tom, knowing without batting an eyelid that he was going to win all of his races, or almost all. Danny was participating in only one of the races, and without thinking twice, Tom also placed a bet on him. This was their first time at the races, and so most of the other people must have thought of them as crazy placing such ridiculously huge bets on their races.

"Well, guys, this is it, most of these people think that we must be out of our heads placing bets on our team, but we know that we can do it. I have given you guys the necessary training and I expect you to pull through successfully and bring a good name back to our stables," Valerie said, rubbing down one of the horses affectionately.

"I'm feeling a little nervous, and especially since I am in so many races, but I think once the races begin, it will go away," Tom said, mounting eagle and then trotting around.

"What about you, Danny, you don't look too enthusiastic about it all, what is the matter?" Valerie turned to Daniel.

"I don't know, Valerie, I feel as if I rushed into this, but I'm keeping my fingers crossed," Danny said, mounting his Arabian black stallion.

"Just have faith and confidence in yourself and you will make it, my boy."

The races soon began and Tom was in the first race. Danny watched as he rode his white stallion to the starting point of the race, and the moment that the gun went off, Tom was amongst the first three of the racers. It was a tight race mainly dominated by one of the older veterans in the horse race industry. At the last moment, almost a hundred meters to the finishing point, Eagle broke loose from the rest of the horses, taking the lead and steadily widening the gap until Tom won the race. There were mostly jeers from the part of the crowd that had bet against him, but Valerie and Danny were over the moon. Valerie jumped up so high, Danny thought he would touch the sky, and Danny could see the same pride that was reflected in his own eyes in Valerie's. They had finally began to make it in the industry, a dream come true for Tom and everyone else. Victory was the name of the game for all the other races that Tom participated in and it was finally time for Danny to race.

"Well, Danny, I believe in you, and I know that you are going to do us proud," Valerie said as Danny mounted his horse.

"Thank you, Valerie, where is Tom, I need his blessing for this race," Danny said, looking down at Tom.

"Tom has just finished his race and might not be able to come here right away, you had better get going, I'm sure that he is praying for you. Go on, now, go," Valerie replied, patting the back of the black stallion.

Daniel rode off feeling unsettled. He would have felt much better if he had seen Tom before the race, sort of a good luck sort of charm. Daniel began riding towards the starting point of the tracks, just as another rider rode up to him.

"Well, well, well, what do we have here, a black rider," the rider sneered as Daniel turned to look at him. It was a skinny red head rider with a southern accent. "And you have come to challenge the big dogs of the game like me, what makes you think that you will win, since I can see that most of the bets for this race have been placed on your horse?"

"Maybe that is because this black rider is going to beat your ass in this race," Danny sneered back at the man, hating his racist sort of attitude.

"Well, black man, we are going to see about that, because nobody beats Johnnie at the steeple chase races."

Daniel ignored the guy and rode his horse to his starting lane, this time more determined than ever to win the race despite the threat that had been in the man's voice. His Arabian stallion was nervously looking forward to the race, and Danny made the horse relax as they waited for the gun to go off. This time more than ever he wanted to win this race if just to show that racist that winning the race was not about the color of the skin, but the talent and professionalism of the jockey. He adjusted his helmet and readied himself for the race, and the minute that the gun went off, Danny was at the lead, steering his stallion clear of the rest with the red head a few feet behind him. He used all of the expertise that he had learned, the first lap completing with him in the lead. Glad for the intensive training that he had given his horse, Danny led on the group of riders, and he could hear the red head cursing his horse for not moving fast enough. Just as he crossed the finish line in the lead, the red head caught up with him and pushed him off his horse. As he fell off the horse, his hand got entangled in the reins, and the horse dragged him through the air and onto the ground. The last thing that Danny remembered was his world turning upside down and a sharp pain as his body hit the ground.

CHAPTER 24

Tom watched as Danny won the race and then he saw the red head pushing him off his horse.

"Noooo," he screamed, jumping over the rails and running towards the finish line to the spot where Daniel lay unconscious.

Security personnel ran to him, restraining him from going to the scene of the accident. He felt as if his life had just come to an end, and Tom watched as Daniel was carried into an ambulance and ferried away. The cops had in the meantime caught the red head, who was arguing furiously saying it had been an accident, and Tom vowed that he would make the man's life a living hell. Tom hurried over to where the cops were holding the red head.

"You asshole, what the hell did you do to Danny?" Tom said, lashing out at the red head and even managing to throw a blow into his cheek. "You bitter good for nothing loser."

"Sir, please, we are going to ask you to step away, we are taking care of him, and we can assure you that this man here will be locked up for a very long time," one of the cops pushed Tom away.

Tom was still there when one of the renown stable owners came over fuming red, addressing the red head. "You stupid fool, what have you done, you have just ruined my business?" he fumed. "Johnnie, I swear to God I'll never forgive you, and I'm going to skin you alive."

The so called Johnnie was escorted to a waiting police car and forced into the back. Tom felt as if his mind had come to a standstill, and for the first time, he did not know what to do. Valerie came to his help and led him to a waiting car.

"Come on, the ranch hands will take care of the horses, we had better go and see how Danny is doing," Valerie said, opening the back door for Tom, who could still not come to terms with the tragedy, and especially since his parents had also died in an accident, although it had been a car accident.

"I'm gonna kill that mother fucker with my bare hands if anything serious has happened to Danny," Tom said, sinking into the chair as Valerie sat beside him.

"It is okay, Danny is a strong guy, and I know that he is going to pull through this," Valerie said, as the chauffeur put the vehicle into gear.

Arriving the hospital reminded Tom of the painful death of his parents, and he felt as if someone was knifing him right in the middle of the heart. The place was busy as usual, as Tom and Valerie rushed over to the reception.

"Pardon me, miss, we are looking for a dark skinned man who was injured at the race tracks today and brought in by an ambulance not very long ago," Valerie said quickly.

"Just a moment, sir, what is the patients name?" the polite nurse replied, keying into her computer.

"Daniel Peters is the name of the patient, he is from the Willow Tree Ranch," Tom replied quickly.

"Ah, here we go, Daniel Peters, he was brought in almost half an hour ago and right now he is in surgery," the nurse said, turning to look at both Tom and Valerie, who wore the looks of horror.

"What, surgery? Did the fall hurt him that seriously?" Tom asked, barely able to believe what he was hearing.

"I'm not privy to the details, but the best thing is to wait for the doctor to finish operating on him, and then you can find out from him, first hand. You can have a seat over there, and I'll let you know as soon as the doctor comes out," she said, showing them towards some waiting chairs so that they could make way for the next person in queue.

Reluctantly, Tom and Valerie moved away from the counter towards the seats. Tom could not even remember how many private prayers he said for the love of his life. Valerie sat down while Tom paces the room back and forth. He felt as if he was in some sort of nightmare and decided that he hated hospitals. It was here that he had lost his mother and father, and now it was here that the love of his life was fighting for his life, how ironical life could be. Tom blamed himself for what had happened to Daniel, since Daniel had kept insisting that he did not feel like the races, but Tom had insisted.

"You know what, Valerie, if anything happens to Danny, I'll never be able to forgive myself. It is all my fault, I kept pressurizing him to race even when he objected. I am such an ass hole, I should have sensed that he had a premonition," Tom said, pacing the room, and for the first time in his life longing for a cigarette.

"Listen here, son, you can't blame yourself for what happened out there. It was an act of malice by that Johnnie fellow, and I'm sure that the whole stadium is baying for his blood at this very moment. We had already immerged as the best racers and he became jealous. Daniel is going to be okay, might just be a couple of broken bones," Valerie said, although from the look on his face, Tom could see that the older man was also very worried, and especially since he treated Danny as if he were his own son.

It was several long hours before the doctor finally made his way out of the surgery room, and as he made his way to the reception, the nurse there pointed towards Tom and Valerie. The doctor walked towards them, pulling off his surgical gloves.

"Are you here for Mr. Daniel Peters?" he asked.

"Yes doctor, how is he?" Tom asked quickly as Valerie stood up.

"He was very badly injured and is in a very delicate state," the doctor said. "Are you relatives of his?"

"Yes, doctor, he is like a son to me, I raised him," Valerie said. "How bad is it? Can we see him?"

"If you will please follow me to my office, I will explain to you everything," the doctor said.

Panic filled him, and his heart was pounding wildly in his chest as Tom followed the doctor and Valerie through the corridor to an office. He kept his fingers crossed and hoped that it was not as serious as the doctor was making it seem. Surely, it was just a fall, and nothing like the car accident that his parents had suffered not too long ago.

"Well, doctor, tell us, what is wrong with him, what is so serious about his condition?" Tom asked as the doctor shut the door and showed them to some chairs infront of a desk.

"Daniel suffered a very bad fall, but luckily, there are no broken bones. He did however injure his spine quite a bit, and I cannot tell for now when he will be able to walk again. We need to wait for him to recover from the surgery and begin physiotherapy. That is a very delicate situation, and only time can tell if he will ever be able to walk again. All hope, however, is not lost, because many people have made it out of similar situations and gotten their bodies back to normal," the doctor said, walking around the desk and settling into a chair.

"Surely, doctor, there has to be something that can be done about it, money is not a problem at all. We can get him the best surgeons if need be," Tom said, a frown forming on his face as his worry threatened to drown him.

"I don't think that we will need other surgeons, because we have very qualified doctors here. What he needs now is plenty of rest and special attention to make sure that he is recuperating well," the doctor said, looking from Tom to Valerie.

"Can we see him right now?" Valerie asked.

"Right now he is asleep, but if you can come back in a couple of hours you will be able to see him," the doctor replied.

"Doctor, can we at least just take a look at him right now and then come back to see him when he wakes up," Tom said urgently and not ready to leave without seeing Danny.

"Maybe we can make an exception for you since this all happened so suddenly," the doctor said, getting up. "Follow me."

Tom felt as if he had just died as they followed the doctor down a corridor and up an elevator to the floor above. They walked down a corridor, coming to a stop outside a door. The doctor opened the door, and Valerie and Tom fearfully stepped into the room. Tom lifted his eyes at the bed, and there was Daniel with drips and an oxygen mask over his face, looking more vulnerable than Tom had ever seen him. He seemed so weak and fragile, Tom immediately felt like going over to him and hugging him, holding him tightly and telling him that everything was going to be okay, but he could not.

"Danny," Tom said in a low voice as Valerie walked over to where he was and put a comforting hand around his shoulder, almost as if he could tell that Tom was at the lowest ebb of his life.

"It is okay, son," he whispered to Tom. "I think that we had better leave and come back later when Danny has had some rest."

"But why, Valerie, why did it have to happen to Danny? Why wasn't it me that fell off the horse?" Tom could no longer hold back his tears and they came pouring down like a shower.

"No, Tom, don't say that, it is okay, Danny is going to be just fine, okay, he is going to be just fine," Valerie said, leading him out of the room as the doctor looked at them skeptically.

"Should I give him a sedative or something?" the doctor asked.

"No, doctor, he will be fine, all that he needs is a little rest to get over this tragic news," Valerie said as he led Tom out of the hospital.

CHAPTER 25

Valerie was very worried, and not only for Danny, but also for Tom. It had been a few hours since they had arrived back at the ranch house, and Tom seemed to have sunk into depression, making Valerie wonder why he had not left him at the hospital in the hands of specialists. Valerie hurried up to Tom's bedroom with a mug of warm chocolate, hoping that it would make him feel better. He wanted to go back into the city to check on Danny, but first he wanted to make sure that Tom was alright. He had slipped a sedative into the chocolate and was hoping that Tom would get some sleep while he was away. he intended to slip away without telling him that he was going back to the hospital, which was probably best. It would be better if Tom were to visit Danny tomorrow since he would probably feel much better.

"Here, Tom, this should make you feel better, you have not eaten anything all afternoon," Valerie said, handing Tom the mug. "The chocolate will surely make you feel better, drink up."

"Thank you, Valerie," Tom said, taking the mug and sipping from it. "Do you think that Danny will be okay? I'm gonna skin that brat who pushed him off his horse."

"Danny is a strong kid, he will get through it," Valerie replied.

"And when he does, I promise to take good care of him. I'll never let him do anything that his heart is not into, never," Tom said, hungrily wolfing down the chocolate and making Valerie wonder why he had not brought him food instead, since Sophia, the cook, had some fried chicken and baked potatoes hot and ready in the kitchen.

"I know that you will, my boy, and so will I. I love you all like you were my very own children, and I watched you both growing up, and if anything bad were to happen to any of you, I would blame myself for having not taken good care of you, and especially since I made a promise to your dad, Mr. Thomas," Valerie said, settling into a seat as Tom laid on his bed.

"Thank you, Valerie, I don't know what I would ever be able to have done without you. After mom and dad died, you took care of me and taught me what I needed to know about the business, and now when Danny is in hospital, you are still by my side, almost as if my dad never left me," Tom said, yawning loudly as the sedative began to kick in.

"Come on, get some rest, and in the morning we can go and visit Danny to see how he is doing, how does that sound?" Valerie asked, although he doubted if Tom even heard him, because he heard him snoring softly. "Good, now I've got to go."

He left the room and went down to the kitchen, where Sophia was seated on a chair weeping.

"How is he, did he go to sleep already?" she asked as Valerie walked into the room.

"Yes, he is asleep, he really needs the rest, everything is happening just too fast for him," Valerie said.

"Poor thing, why do all of these tragedies have to happen to this family like this, first his folks and now Danny! I feel so very sorry for him, and for you too, Valerie, I know that this is like your family too," she said softly, getting up and beginning to serve him food.

"Sophia, we are all family here, including you, and we should always stand together. We might not be related by blood, but we are related by love and affection, is that understood?" Valerie said, getting up and hugging Sophia warmly.

"Yes," she said, beginning to sob in his arms.

Valerie let her cry and when she was done, he dug into his chicken and potatoes and then headed back to the hospital. Danny was awake but in no state to talk, his eyes looking at Valerie as if he was not looking at him.

"Danny, I'm so glad that you are awake, how are you feeling?" Valerie said softly, walking to the side of the bed and touching Danny's hand.

Danny moved his fingers, and Valerie could only imagine the sort of pain that he was going through. Valerie sat on the chair next to the bed wondering what was happening to all of the people that he loved as family.

CHAPTER 26

Danny felt like hell. From the moment that he had woken up, he had felt as if he had just been in a bomb blast. His body ached everywhere as he tried to recall what had happened at the tracks. He remembered the threat from the red head, the race and even the curses of the red head behind him, and then he remembered winning the race just as someone pushed him off his horse. He could not remember how he got here, wherever it was, but as his eyes fluttered open, Danny realized that he was in some sort of hospital room and there were pipes and drips all over. His eyes were all blurry and his body ached all over. He tried to raise his head but it was as heavy as lead and could not move. He then realized that he even had on an oxygen mask and he could not move his hands and legs. They felt lifeless, almost as if they did not exist, and it made Danny panic.

He felt as if half of his body was dead, and the only part of his body working his mind and now his eyes. There was a sound in the room, and when Danny moved his eyes, into the room walked Valerie accompanied by a nurse. Never in his life had he felt so helpless before because he wanted to ask Valerie what was happening and where Tom was but he could not. Now more than ever, Danny wanted to get better. He wanted his life to get back to normal, and for the first time realized the beauty of life. He realized the beauty of good health and the beauty of loving and being loved. For now all that he could do was to watch and listen helplessly.

CHAPTER 27

Tom held Danny in his arms as they kissed deeply and passionately. Their cocks were both hard, and Tom took his hand down Danny's naked body to his crotch, beginning to rub his hand over his dick. Tom felt his own cock pulsating with desire as Danny too took his hand down to Tom's dick and wrapped his fingers around it, beginning to jerk it up and down. Both men were standing in the shallow end of the swimming pool at the back of the ranch house after a swim to cool their bodies off. It had been a straining day at the ranch and now under the afternoon sun, Danny and Tom were unwinding. Danny then lifted Tom off the ground and carried him out of the water, their lips never leaving each other. Danny carried Tom to one of the pool beds and placed him onto his back. Pulling his lips away from Tom's, Danny moved down to Tom's waist and crouched beside the pool bed. Tom held his breath, looking down at Danny as Danny sniffed in his clean shaved crotch. He then watched Tom's dark lips encompassing the pink head of his dick as Danny began sucking on it. Tom closed his eyes, taking his hands down to Danny's clean shaved head and beginning to massage it as Danny began taking more and more of the male flesh into his mouth. Tom felt his balls beginning to burn with desire, the heat within them threatening to explode.

Tom held Danny's head still and then began driving his dick in and out of Danny's mouth, mouth fucking him. Tom pushed his cock as deep as it could go into Danny's mouth, and he could hear Danny grunting as the thickness forced its way into his mouth. Tom's balls tightened in their sac as an intense need to release arose in them. He felt as if he had died and gone to heaven, and was being rewarded by God as the intensity of the pleasure increased. All of the goose bumps on his forearms had sprung to life as the sensations of the friction of his dick against the walls of Danny's mouth drove him crazy. Suddenly, Tom felt a knot forming in the pit of his stomach, an overwhelming heat in his balls as his dick exploded into a huge orgasm. His balls tightened even more, a groan escaping from his throat as his seed shot into Danny's mouth. Tom drove his cock deep into Danny's mouth, sending his jism down Danny's throat.

Suddenly, all of the pleasure came to an end, and when Tom opened his eyes, he realized that he was alone in bed. His semen had spoofed over his sheets and he could still feel the heat leaving his balls. He realized with disgust that it had all been a wet dream, a wet dream that just left him craving for more. As reality began to sink in, Tom remembered that Danny was not even at the house with them, but was still in hospital. Wondering for how long he had slept, Tom got out of bed quickly and checked his phone. It was morning and he must have slept quite heavily and had missed going back to the hospital in the evening. Eager to see his lover, Tom quickly made his way to the bathroom for a quick shower. He still felt groggy, probably from sleeping too much, and he was also very hungry since he had not eaten all afternoon yesterday. After showering, Tom changed into clothes quickly and made his way downstairs, heading straight to the kitchen.

"Hello, Tom," Sophia greeted as he walked into the kitchen, where she was busy brewing coffee and making ham and cheese sandwiches. "How are you feeling today, my child, you must be hungry."

"I'm starving, Sophia, what do we have for breakfast, and where is Valerie?" Tom said, hugging her warmly and then settling onto a chair.

"I prepared some sandwiches, although I could fix you something a little heavier if you wish," she replied sweetly. "Valerie must be somewhere around, I saw him heading towards the stables, probably checking to see if everything is going well."

"Is there any news from the hospital on Danny's condition?" Tom asked as Sophia put a plate of sandwiches before him.

"Well, Valerie went there last night, but there was no improvement. My Danny was just lying there on the hospital bed helplessly and even unable to talk," Sophia said, looking saddened as she conveyed the news.

"He should have woken me up. Anyways, I'm going over there right now," Tom said, biting into a sandwich and then sipping from his mug of coffee.

"May the good Lord take care of that poor soul, he does not deserve to be like that," Sophia said, settling on the chair opposite Tom at the dining table.

"That is very true, you can imagine how I feel, Sophia, and what makes it suck even more is the fact that I'm the one who coerced him into racing. I am guilty for the way that he is, and it should have been me at the hospital instead," Tom said, his heart heavy with guilt.

"Don't say things like that, my son, you cannot blame yourself for what happened, it is the fault of the nut who pushed my poor little Danny off his horse," Sophia said to him consolingly.

"Yeah, and talking of that red head, I'm going by the precinct just to make sure that he has not gotten away. I want to make sure that he rots in prison," Tom said bitterly, just as Valerie walked into the kitchen.

"Good morning and how did you sleep, Tom," he said, getting a mug and pouring himself some coffee.

"I'm fine, Valerie, where the hell have you been, we should have left already, and especially since you did not wake me up last night," Tom replied.

"Well, I had to go and check things around the ranch just to make sure that everything is going as expected," Valerie said, before sipping on the coffee. "As for the hospital, visitors are not allowed until one in the afternoon. You will have to find something to keep you busy until then."

"In that case, I would like to get the best lawyer that we can get so that we can prosecute and sue the red head. I'm going to make him regret ever coming into this world, and if he is jailed, I would like you to get in touch with the prison warders so that I can make sure that he has the worst time of his life in there. He is going to regret ever bringing harm to someone that I love," Tom said bitterly as anger began to course through his veins. "If the same were to happen to any of you, Sophia, the only family that I have left, I would not hesitate to do the same."

"Okay then, we had better get going to the precinct if that is where you wanna go," Valerie said, finishing up his coffee and standing up to take his mug to the sink.

"Yeah, we had better get going. I think that it is actually better, since I am actually frightened of going to the hospital. I want some news on the red head before I head to the hospital," Tom said, also getting up and beginning to follow Valerie out of the kitchen. "Thank you for the breakfast, Sophia, I'll see you later."

"May God go with you, son," she replied, just before he closed the door behind them.

CHAPTER 28

Tom was eager to get news on the red head as they got to the precinct. He got out of the car even before Valerie managed to get a free parking, and dashed up the stairs and into the building. He dashed to the reception, where there was a guard on duty.

"Hi, how can I help you?" the middle aged cop asked.

"Hello, I'm here regarding a guy who was brought here yesterday for pushing a rider off his horse," Tom said quickly.

"Are you his lawyer?" the cop asked.

"No, that man crippled someone who is very special to me and I would like to make sure that he rots in jail," Tom said bitterly just as Valerie walked into the building.

"And I totally agree with him," the Frenchman said.

"Well, you won't have a problem with that because Johnnie will be locked away for a very long time. There are several witnesses and there is even video footage showing everything that happened. We are going to make him a lesson to all the other people who think like him," the police chief said, walking out of an adjoining office. "It is nice to see you, Mr. Sharpe. I'm Brendan Cole, the chief of police here. Those were some very good moves that you made yesterday winning all of those races like you did."

"Thank you, chief. It is good to know that you are also into horse racing since I know that you will ensure justice for my friend," Tom said, shaking the chief's hand firmly.

"You can count on me for that, I witnessed the whole thing, and I think that it is a real shame to do that to your opponents no matter how much they are kicking your ass," the chief said, motioning for Tom and Valerie to follow him into his office. "Can I have your autograph, my wife will really be excited when I show it to her?"

"Sure," Tom said, taking the baseball bat and marker pen that the chief handed him and signing on the bat, the results of his recent fame beginning to show openly. "There you go, chief."

"I'm glad that we finally have the issue of the red head under wraps and I can sleep easy," Valerie said. "Think we should be heading to the hospital to check on Danny new?"

"Yes, Valerie, that is the next thing on our agenda, let us get going," Tom said. "Thank you very much for your time, chief, but we had better get down to the hospital to see Daniel."

"That is fine, I'll pass by there later to see if I can take a statement from Mr. Peters," the chief said, getting up and walking them to the door of his office as they left.

Tom felt his stomach churning as they drove to the hospital. He was anxious and praying that Daniel was going to be alright, because he would never forgive himself if something bad happened to him. He was going to take the full blame because he is the one who had pressurized him to take part in the race. He was quiet in the drive across the town, worry fogging his mind. Valerie seemed to notice that and he tried to bring up some idle conversation, but it was not working for Tom. He had a bad feeling about the whole scenario and he blamed himself for everything. It was visiting hours by the time that they got to the hospital, and it was bustling with people, almost impossible to get around, as people came to visit their patients. Valerie led Tom through the corridors to the wing where Danny was, but when they pushed the door open, there was just an empty bed and no Daniel. Panic filled him so much, Tom could not talk. Had the worst already happened to Danny and he no longer existed in this world?

"Valerie, where is Danny?" he managed to croak.

"Yesterday he was right here," Valerie replied, his voice filled with worry that reflected Tom's.

"What if... what if he is...." Tom said, breaking down as he began crying bitterly for his departed lover.

"Are you two here to visit Mr. Daniel Peters?" a nurse asked, and Valerie nodded at him. "I'm sorry-"

Tom collapsed onto the floor not able to listen to the rest of the sentence that the nurse had to say. The last thing he remembers was hitting the ground and then everything went dark. Suddenly he was floating on the clouds, walking towards some huge gates that had angels on the inside. Could this be heaven, and was Daniel already here? There was a man dressed in white seated on the inner side of the gate, probably angel Gabriel waiting to welcome him through the pearly gates.

CHAPTER 29

Valerie hurried to Tom's side and crouched down as the nurse finished her sentence.

"I'm sorry he is not here, there was a slight improvement in his situation, and he was taken in for a couple of tests," she completed.

"Help, I think Tom must have gone into some state of shock or something," Valerie said, holding Tom's wrist to check his pulse.

The nurse rang a bell and seconds later the whole room was teaming with nurses.

"We are going to have to ask you to step aside, sir, so that we can check him out," a doctor said, walking into the room and signaling for a nurse to take Valerie out of the room as Tom was put onto a stretcher.

Worry was killing him as he stepped out of the room. Tragedy after tragedy seemed to be happening to the only people that he loved, one minute that, and the next this. He watched as Tom was pushed out of the room, the nurses practically running, and an oxygen mask already over his face. Valerie dashed after them, but they disappeared into the emergency room and closed the doors in his face. Frustrated, he walked back to Daniel's room and began pacing up and down as he wondered what had happened to Tom. He prayed to God that it was not a cardiac arrest or something as horrific as that. He had probably fallen into some state of shock and would come around as soon as they gave him something to deal with it. A few minutes later, Daniel was whisked into the room on a wheel chair, looking much better than he had looked yesterday. Valerie saw recognition in his eyes, and Daniel smiled at him warmly as he entered the room.

"Daniel," Valerie said warmly, glad to see that at least not all was lost.

"Valerie," Daniel managed to whisper. "Tom, where is Tom?"

For the first time in his life, Valerie was at a loss of what to say. He did not want to burden Daniel with the sad news that Tom had just suffered from some sort of shock because of him, although he knew that the truth would eventually come to life.

"Daniel, I'm so glad that you are looking much better now, it is a miracle, yesterday you were like a cabbage, helpless," Valerie said, walking over to Daniel quickly and hugging him softly before the nurses helped him onto the bed.

"Tom, Valerie, where is Tom?" Daniel said.

"Well, we actually came with him to visit you, but he got some sort of complication and the doctors took him in for checkup," Valerie said, choosing his words carefully.

"Complications?" Danny said, surprising the nurse as he sat up on his own.

"Sir, I think you had better get down and rest, your body is still very weak from all the medication," one of the nurses said, trying to push him back onto his back.

"No, I wanna go and see Tom, what is wrong with him? He is the only reason that I got to get the will to live again, and the main reason that I'm alive right not. I therefore really have to see him," Daniel said stubbornly.

"Danny, Tom is with the doctors right now in the emergency room, and visitors are not allowed to see him just yet, maybe after the doctors are done checking him out. Right now I need for you to rest like the nurse said, and once Tom is available, we can go and visit him," Valerie said.

CHAPTER 30

Daniel could not believe what was happening. He felt as if his whole life had just come to an end and there was no longer the need to live. He wondered what was happening to Tom, a guy who had been so healthy and vibrant only yesterday. He lay back on his bed and said a silent prayer for his love, praying that it was nothing serious. Could Tom have gone into shock because of him? Daniel was still lying there wondering why life had to be so stubborn at times, when one of the doctors walked into the room.

"Are you the one who came in with the young man?" the doctor asked Valerie, and from the look on his face, things did not seem too good.

"Yes doctor, his name is Tom, Tom Langley Sharpe III, and I'm Valerie. What is wrong with my boy? Is he going to be alright?" Valerie said quickly as Daniel struggled to sit up on the bed.

"Well, Tom suffered a severe attack of shock," the doctor said.

"What do you mean by that?" Daniel asked quickly.

"You have just had a miraculous recovery that has left all of the doctors here baffled, and I think you should get some rest," the doctor said to Daniel. "I have never seen such a recovery."

"Well, I came back to good health because I wanted to be with Tom," Daniel said, smiling weakly at the doctor. "How is he, doctor, what do you mean by severe attack of shock?"

"Tom went into a coma, I think whatever it was that shocked him got to him in a bad way," the doctor said.

"A coma? Will he be able to come through from it? Isn't there anything that you can do, because I'm not leaving this hospital without Tom," Danny said, suddenly feeling as if he had healed and the only thing that mattered being Tom's recovery.

"Comas are very delicate situations. He might pull through it but it might have its side effects. Depending on his will power, he might come back with a full memory. In other circumstances, he might take time to recover his memory, or worse still, never get his memory back. It is all really up to God, and so is the time that he will be in a coma. People have been known to remain in comas for years," the doctor said.

Daniel took the news like a horror story, almost as if it was not actually happening. Daniel wondered what he had done to God to deserve this, and now more than ever, he was determined to be healed, just so that he could be strong for Tom. Tom was everything to him, he was his life, and Daniel could not imagine living life without him there. This was just a rough patch of their lives, and Daniel was more than ever convinced that they were going to get through it. If ever there was a time when Daniel needed God to come through for him, it was right now.

CHAPTER 31

It had been exactly one month since Tom had been admitted to the hospital, and still there was no improvement in his condition. He had been in a coma, lying there almost lifeless, and Daniel had never left his side for a minute, save for the times he visited the washrooms. The doctors and even Valerie had pleaded with him to go home and wait for the day they would give him the news that Tom was finally out of his coma, but he would never hear of it. He talked to Tom even though Tom could not hear him, constantly reminding him that he needed for him to come back to life so that they could continue with their beautiful life. He even had Valerie bring books that he would read to Tom, believing that Tom could somehow hear him within the recesses of his mind. He knew that Tom was a strong willed man and he was going to come through. This time, Daniel promised himself that he was going to take good care of Tom, the sort of care that he deserved. What he needed was for him to come out of his coma, the coma that he did not deserve.

Danny thought back about his own life. He was subjected to a wheelchair for God knows how long because of the injury he got on his back, but the doctors said that with the right amount of therapy and practice, he could get better and even walk pretty soon. Danny might have already begun walking, but he had postponed his own therapy so that he could be by Tom's side, taking good care of him. The moment that he saw that Tom was out of any sort of danger, he would do his best to get his life back into normal working order.

CHAPTER 32

Tom felt himself floating towards the pearly gates. He had been floating a long while, and he wondered why he had not yet spotted Danny. Could Daniel have already gone past the gates? He was not sure, because behind him he could hear a familiar voice calling him.

"Tom, please come back, it is Danny, and I need for you to come back, I need you. I need you right now more than ever, please do not leave me alone in this world," Daniel's voice echoed over and over again, making Tom stop on his cloud.

He turned around and began heading back from where he had come, where the voice was coming from. He began running fast as the voice became louder. His Danny was not dead, he was alive, and the nurse had lied to him. He wished that his stallion, Eagle, was here so that he could get to Danny faster. Suddenly he coughed and when he opened his eyes, there was Daniel seated on a wheelchair next to him, holding his hands.

"Danny, is that you?" he asked, coughing.

"Yes, Tom, it is me, thank God you came back," Danny said excitedly, kissing Tom's hand before turning his wheelchair around. "Doctor, he is awake, Tom is awake."

Doctors and nurses ran into the room, all looking very surprised.

"What happened?" Tom asked, confused and surprised when he discovered that he was in a hospital bed.

"You have been in a coma, Tom," the doctor said, examining him with a stethoscope.

Coma? Tom could not believe that he had been in a coma, because he felt as if he had probably fallen asleep and had been dreaming that he was going to heaven. Tom tried to raise his head off the bed, but found that he could not, almost as if his head had become as heavy as lead.

"Please, sir, try and relax, you have been in a coma for a month and your muscles are very stiff," the doctor said, pushing him back onto the bed. "We are going to have to take a few tests on you just to make sure that you are good to go, and then we can assign you a therapist to help with your muscles."

"Does this mean that he is healed, doctor?" Daniel said, trying to jump up with joy and falling to the ground infront of the wheelchair.

"Daniel, what do you think you are doing, you know that you are not yet in a position to walk?" the doctor said as nurses helped Daniel back onto his chair.

"I know doctor, but if Tom has woken up, I believe that I'm going to be walking very soon," Daniel said with determination that made Tom also want to get out of his bed as soon as possible.

"You have a very dedicated friend here, Tom, you are one hell of a lucky guy," the doctor turned back to Tom. "He never left your side for a minute and even slept on his wheel chair."

"I-I thought that Danny had died," Tom said softly, afraid to even mention death.

"Nope, you are the one who came very close to death, I really wonder how you managed to come back," one of the nurses marveled as she adjusted a drip.

"I had a dream. I was walking towards huge pearly gates above the clouds when I heard Danny telling me to come back. I turned and began running back, and when I woke up, here I was," Tom said, almost as if it was a dream that not even he would believe.

"I think that it is a miracle that you are awake, it means that we almost lost your soul," the doctor said as he began taking a number of tests.

Exhausted from the effort of talking, Tom lay back and let the doctor do his thing, feeling the muscles on his body as well as asking him to do things like breathe in and out, or wiggle his fingers and toes. Tom fell asleep and this time the dream was of good things that were alive. He dreamed of the good things that he intended to have with Daniel. He was alive and that was all that mattered. In his dream, Daniel was not a cripple but running and walking as usual, and they made love whenever they got the chance, their love even more alive than it had ever been. After all of the trials and tribulations, it was only fair that they lived their lives to the full and cherished the love that they felt for each other.

CHAPTER 33

The plans for the home coming party had kept Daniel pretty busy, despite the fact that he was still riding on a wheelchair. He hurried around the mansion, ensuring that the organizers had brought in everything that he and Valerie had asked for.

"I don't think you should be straining yourself like this," Valerie said as Daniel wheeled into the kitchen, inspecting the food that Sophia had prepared for the bash.

"I feel as if this is the most important day of my life, almost as if I am getting a chance to live again. Tom has been out of the house for over a month and I expect a grand welcome," Daniel said, wheeling around the kitchen.

"I still think that you should let Valerie and I handle the preparations," Sophia said, a smile on her face for the first time in a long time.

"Sitting down doing nothing is not going to help me one bit, I need to be active, doctor's orders," Daniel smiled at her, joy filling his heart with all of the love that was going around. "As for you, Valerie, I think you should get going to pick Tom up already. I wish I could come with you, but it is too cumbersome with this wheelchair."

"Yes, Valerie, go on and bring my Tom back home, how I have missed him so," Sophia said.

"Alright, I'm going, just let me grab my coat and I'll be out of here before you know it," Valerie said, walking out of the kitchen, and a few minutes later, Daniel heard the trucks engines firing to life, almost as if they were bringing him a new life.

Daniel had the feeling that this was the beginning of something new and exciting, more exciting than it had ever been, even though it would take time for everything to quite get back to normal.

"I am so excited that things around the ranch will now get back to normal with you and Tom back at the house. I had really missed having you both here, and I missed you dearly," Sophia said, settling onto a dining seat.

"I missed you too, Sophia, and I'm sure that Tom also missed you very much, he has been asking us about you every single day, since he came out of the coma," Daniel said, spinning his wheelchair around and heading out of the kitchen. "I'll try and see if I can freshen myself up a little, it has been a crazy morning."

"Well, you let me know if there is anything that you need," Sophia shouted after him as Daniel made his way to his new bedroom on the ground floor landing of the mansion.

Daniel had moved back to the ranch house a few days ago, soon after Tom had come out of his coma. He had devised ways of efficiently doing things without having to ask for help unless it was absolutely necessary. He busied himself in the bedroom. For some reason, today he was feeling extremely excited, not only because Tom was coming back home, but also because he had gone for quite a while without having sex, and he was looking forward to it. He was incapacitated from the waist downwards, but Daniel believed that where there was a way, there was a will, and they would find a way of making their passion come alive. Since the day that Tom had gotten out of his coma, Daniel had found himself waking up with an aching hard on every morning, and all that he could think of was making love. At times he wondered if Tom felt the same way since he had never gathered the guts yet to ask him. Daniel wanted Tom to become fine before he began making such demands, and luckily, Tom was doing very well, and had even began walking around in his hotel room. If he could do that, who knows what else he could do, deliciously naughty things, that is.

Thinking about sex, Daniel felt his dick becoming hard in his pants, a huge tent forming in there. Without thinking twice, Daniel pushed his hand into the waist of his pants and past his boxers to take a hold of his manhood. Wrapping his fingers around his thickness, Daniel began jerking his dick up and down slowly, imagining that it was Tom doing it for him. Daniel closed his eyes, letting his imagination roam as he imagined Tom's white lips wrapping around the dark head of his dick as he began to suck on it, rubbing his tongue over the tip and spreading the precum that had already formed there over the sensitive head deliciously. Daniel began groaning out in pleasure as Tom began taking more and more of his dick into his mouth, his head bobbing up and down over his ebony cock.

Daniel found himself jerking his cock hard, moving his waist up and down as he imagined his dick going deeper and deeper into Tom's mouth. His arousal was so intense, his desire so pent up, Daniel felt his balls burning, just as his cock erupted, sending his seed deep into Tom's mouth. Daniel was panting by the time that he opened his eyes and realized that he had just spoofed in his pants in what was one of the most intensive hand jobs of his life. Breathing heavily from the intensity of the orgasm, Daniel pulled his cum stained hand out of his pants and brought it up to his mouth, getting a taste of his male juices. He licked his fingers clean and then pulled his pants open so that he could assess the amount of erotic damage in his pants. Quite a huge mess, he was going to have to change into some other clothes and make a point of tossing his clothes into the washing machine. Slowly, he struggled out of his pants and boxers and then put on a pair of fresh clothes. He could still feel the effects of his climax as he finally made his way out of the room.

CHAPTER 34

Tom was elated. He had not expected to find such a huge party waiting for him at home, and all of his friend's and the ranch workers were around. The one person who graced the party though, was Daniel. He looked superb, almost like some sort of sex God that got his body on fire without even touching him. Tom had a hard time fending off women who had always had a crush on him, and some who had realized just how handsome he was after he had won the race. Maybe in another life, but right now the only person that Tom wanted to have any kind of relationship with was Danny. Being in the walls of the hospital had made him feel like a prisoner, and it felt so good to be back home.

There was a constant itch in his pants, and Tom found that he had a hard on that he could not get rid of. Was it humanly possible for a man to feel so randy? He was lucky to have a huge jacket that covered his clothes since he did not want to imagine the looks on the guests faces when they realized how hot and horny he was. Checking around and seeing that Daniel was busy with some of the guests, Tom sneaked out of the room, eager to get somewhere where he could jerk off. At least maybe that could hold it out until when he was alone with Danny later on. He made his way across the grounds, heading towards the barn's, a place that he knew was deserted by now since everyone was at the party. Entering one of the barns and feeling way too horny to even remember to close the door, Tom stripped off his pants and then pulled off his boxers as well. Tossing his pants onto a bale of hay, he sat on them, wrapping his fingers around his cock and leaning back with his eyes closed, not noticing Shania, one of the girls who had a mad crush on him following him into the barn and closing the door quietly.

Shania was feeling hotter and hornier than she had ever felt, and she quickly removed her clothes quietly. She was aching in between her thighs, and her pussy had creamed up with need as she tried to imagine how the cock that Tom was jerking so deliciously would feel inside her wet needy cunt. She was trembling with need as she set the camera of her smart phone on so that it could record them, before Shania dipped her hand in between her thighs, her fingers dipping into her needy pussy. She began running her fingers through her wetness, playing them over her throbbing clit. She took the clit in between her forefinger and her thumb and began rolling it around in semi circles, heightening the arousal that she felt. She had always dreamt of watching a man masturbating, and it was the most arousing thing that she had ever seen.

Shania drove her fingers deeper into her cunt, hooking them as she pulled them out, and the hooked digit rubbing pleasantly over her G spot and almost making her to moan out in pleasure. The look on Tom's face was one of pure bliss, his face turning into many different forms as he jerked his hand faster and harder over his dick. His balls had tightened in their sac, and Shania could only imagine the sort of semen that was waiting to explode out of the shaft, cum that she knew would feel very fulfilling inside the depths of her vagina. Her eyes roved over the huge pink slit at the tip of Tom's cock, and there had pooled delicious looking precum that made her mouth water. She felt the heat within her loins increasing as she finger fucked herself in the same fashion that Tom was jerking his cock. If she could not have him in the flesh, then she would have him just like this, while she waited for him to make up his mind over what he wanted in life.

The rumor mill around the town had it that Tom was gay, but that only made him even more appealing. Shania wondered why the most appealing and delicious things always had to be forbidden. She had been in love with Tom since she was in her early teens and right now at 19 she was still just as madly in love with him. She had been saving her virginity for him and hoped that one day he would accord her the sort of attention that she deserved. Shania suddenly felt a knot forming in her belly, just as her cunt contracted over her fingers, her pussy exploding into an orgasm. Shania played her fingers in and out of her cunt furiously just as she watched Tom explode into a climax of his own. His semen shot out from the pink slit at the tip of the cock like molten lava flowing out of an active volcano mountain, rolling over the side and over his fingers. Just then, Tom opened his eyes, his jaw dropping when he saw the naked woman near him with her fingers buried deep in her sex.

"Shania.... What are you doing here?" Tom asked, surprise an understatement.

"Shh, I just came here to masturbate like you. Now, if you don't mind, let me clean you up with my mouth and nobody will ever know what went on in here," Shania said, getting up and moving towards Tom as he sat there frozen. "I'm sure that you don't want to go back to the party with all of this semen smeared over you."

She had a point, and Tom leaned back on the hay as she wrapped her lips around his dick and began sucking on it, running her tongue over the length of the cock. She licked the cock expertly, moping over every inch of the shaft with her wet lips, but sweet as it felt, it did not feel as good as he felt when it was Daniel doing the same thing to him. If there was a woman who loved him with her whole heart, it was Shania, and Tom had the feeling that she could do anything for him. It was a pity that she had to keep her hopes up like this, since Tom did not know if he would ever be able to love anyone else other than Danny. She licked his dick, teasing it and trying to tempt it back to life, and it was only moments before she began to get results. Maybe it was because he had gone for so long without sex, but Tom felt his dick beginning to harden in her mouth, blowing up as it became bigger and bigger until it could no longer fit in her mouth. She finally pulled her mouth off the cock and looked at his face.

"Look here, Tom, I'm sure that by now you know exactly how I feel about you. I have been saving my virginity for you, and if you can just give me this one favor since I know that you probably have no feelings for me. Make love to me, Tom," she whispered, massaging his dick with her fingers, her thumb rubbing over the tip pleasurably. "Make love to me, make me become a woman like all the other women of my age. Show me what it feels like to make love."

Tom could read the need in her voice, and the fact that he had gone for quite a while without erotic pleasure got him highly turned on. Making out with her just once surely would not hurt, and besides, she had always been good to him. Without waiting for his answer, Shania climbed on top of him, straddling him by the waist with her sex directly above his dick. She lowered herself down on him, taking a hold of his dick and guiding it into her searing wetness. Not as tight as Danny's ass hole was, but it would do for now. He felt his dick pushing against her hymen, just as she moaned out softly, the cock breaking her virginity. She lowered herself all the way onto him until his cock was fully inserted in her cunt, and then she leaned forward, placing her hands on his shoulders as she began riding him. The sliminess of the pussy juices against his dick felt delicious, and Tom began to feel desire raging within him.

He held her y the hips and supported her as she rode him faster and harder, taking his dick in and out of her vagina in long strokes. Tom looked down and saw the mixture of her love juices and her blood on his dick as she rode him furiously. Her breasts moved up and down on her chest, and from the intensity of her breathing, Tom could tell that she was almost climaxing. This was a whole new experience for him, and unable to hold back, he felt his dick stiffening inside her cunt. She suddenly fused her lips hard onto his, kissing him deeply as they both climaxed. She milked his dick with her pussy muscles, her cunt swallowing all of his cum.

Tom used a different route back to the ranch house from the one that Shania used. He could not risk a scandal right now, and it was best if nobody else ever found out what had just happened between them in the barn. It had just been a spur of the moment, and passion had overtaken their line of reason. He hurried upstairs to his bedroom and took a hot shower before he changed into some fresh clothes and made his way back down to the party. He stopped a waiter and picked up a glass of champagne, draining it instantly and setting the glass back on the tray.

"Ah, there you are, where the hell have you been, I've been looking for you all over?" Daniel said, steering his wheelchair towards him.

"I took a breather around the ranch, I had really missed the freedom of being out there," Tom replied, turning to look at Daniel.

"Well, I really missed you and could not wait for you to move back home," Daniel said, looking into Tom's blue eyes. "I missed your voice, your scent, your touch. I missed all of the love that you used to give me, and for a moment there I thought that I had lost you to that coma forever."

"You are making me feel like blushing," Tom said to his friend. "I can't wait to be alone with you later tonight, I intend to do very naughty things with you."

"Ah, here you are, Tom," Valerie said, walking up to them. "The guests are waiting for you to come and toast to your good health and prosperity."

The party seemed to last forever, and Tom was pretty exhausted by the time that the first of the guests began leaving the ranch. He really wanted to hit the sack and look forward to tomorrow, and especially since he had not been up so long in quite a while. Tom found his way to one of the couches in the living room and decided to relax for a while, and the next thing, his sleep had taken over and he was in dreamland.

CHAPTER 35

Daniel woke up with a heavy head. He must have had a little too much to drink during the party last night because his head felt as if he had just been ran over by a truck. He could not even remember how he had gone to bed, or what time the last of the guests had gone, if at all they had all left. He lifted his head off the bed slowly and opened his heavy eyelids. At first he did not quite remember where he was, but as he looked around, he realized that he was in one of the spare bedrooms near the laundry room. Someone had lifted him off his wheelchair and set him on the bed, but that was not all. Whoever it was had also gone ahead and undressed him, leaving him completely naked on the bed, and as he woke up, he realized that he had on a huge erection that was aching with need. Morning wood was what he called it, and it was aching for a release. His eyes travelled around the room to the other bed in the room. He swallowed hard when he saw what was happening on the bed, because there were two male guests of theirs, whose names he could not quite recall, and they were both naked. One of the men was lying on top of the other one in such a way that both men were sucking on each other's morning wood.

Daniel felt a strain in his groin as he ached for such a thing. His reality began to settle in and Daniel wondered where Tom was. How could he have gotten so drunk to the point of forgetting to keep a tab on Tom? What if Tom had needed him for some sort of favor or something of the sort? Daniel tried to get up from the bed and remembered that he was incapacitated from the waist down. He lay back on the bed, frustrated by all of the lust that he was feeling within. The man who was on top of the other guy on the other man, pulled the other man's long slender cock out of his mouth and looked over at Daniel, looking at his hard dark cock and swallowing hard. The man then went back to the cock that he had been sucking on, taking it deep into his mouth, his eyes never leaving Daniel's cock. This was all too much for Daniel, and he took his hand down to his dick, wrapping his fingers around the dark thickness as he began jerking it up and down. He felt his balls burning with need, and the scene next to him was not making things any better. This was torture at its best, and Daniel was not sure if he would be able to handle it for very long.

"Wanna join us mate, we surely wouldn't mind getting you into the action?" the man finally pulled the cock out of his mouth again.

"Not a chance in the world, guys, he is with me," a familiar voice said from the doorway, and when Daniel looked there, Tom was standing in the doorway looking more handsome and appealing than ever, despite the fact that he was fully clothed.

"You heard the man," Daniel said, sitting up on his elbow. "Tom, what the hell took you so long to get here, I feel as if my cock is about to explode?"

"I wanted you fully rested before I came to you, you were pretty drunk last night and I had a hell of a time bringing you in here," Tom said, closing the door behind him and then facing Daniel.

"Well, it is about time," Daniel said excitedly as Tom began unbuttoning his shirt, pulling it off swiftly and tossing it onto a dressing table before he began to unbuckle his belt.

Tom pulled off his pants and then followed with his boxers to reveal the cock that Daniel had fallen in love with right from the very first time he set his eyes on it. Tom's white cock was as hard as granite, and Daniel trembled when he tried to imagine the fact that it would soon be inserted deep within him, ploughing pleasure through his body. He watched Tom walking to the bed slowly, his weight sinking onto the bed as he sat on it and leaned towards Daniel. Their lips went together, fusing tightly as they began kissing deeply and passionately. Daniel's lips parted readily as Tom's tongue pushed into his mouth to begin dancing over his erotically, heightening the desire that he was feeling. Tom reached his hand down to Daniel's dick and wrapped his fingers around it, beginning to jerk it up and down slowly. Daniel trembled with desire, every vein in his body coming alive as it pulsated with desire.

Daniel wanted to feel more than just the kiss, he wanted to taste Tom's dick, and especially since he had really missed the taste of his friend's dick. He pulled his lips away from Tom's and then made Tom get onto his back on the bed. The couple on the other bed in the meantime, were already boning, and one of the men was seated on the bed, while the other one was sort of crouched over him, riding his dick and taking it deep into his butt hole. Watching the way that the men were making love, Danny leaned over Tom, his dark fingers circling his dick as he lowered his mouth down to the crotch, he sniffed in the hairless crotch, the male scent making him dizzy with desire. Feeling more aroused than ever, Daniel wrapped his lips over the tip of the manhood and began sucking on it, playing his tongue over the tip and getting a taste of the delicious precum that he had missed so much.

CHAPTER 36

Tom groaned with desire as Daniel began sucking his dick head, running his tongue deliciously over the sensitive skin. Daniel began taking more and more of the dick into his mouth, his head beginning to move up and down over the white shaft. Tom took his hands down to Daniel's bald head, pressing it harder onto his shaft and forcing more of the manhood into her mouth. Heaven was beyond words of what he was feeling, and his balls were on fire as desire coursed through every vein in his body. He felt the head of his dick slipping into Daniel's throat, and he let out a groan, sure that if he let Daniel continue sucking him off, he was going to come in his mouth. He wanted to come elsewhere and so he pulled Daniel's head off his dick.

"Enough, honey, I wanna come inside you, but not in your mouth," Tom said, pushing Daniel seated as he lowered his head to the massive dark monster cock.

Tom curled his lips around the girth of the cock and began sucking on it, putting most of the concentration on the delicious juices coming out of the love rod. As he sucked on the cock, Tom massaged Danny's huge balls, making them grow taut in their sac. Danny's breathing became even heavier as he took his hands down to Tom's head, pressing it hard against his dick. Daniel pushed his dick deep into Tom's mouth, and Tom felt the pecker stiffening in his mouth, just before a huge load of cum shot into his mouth. Tom gripped his lips around the black cock, sucking and swallowing all of the love juices that Daniel showered into his mouth. As soon as Danny was done coming, Tom pulled his mouth off the cock and then got up, making Daniel to lie on his front side. Tom then parted Daniel's butt cheeks and ran his tongue through it, bringing it to a stop on the butt hole.

Tom eased his tongue into the butt hole, parting it slowly as memories of all the pleasure that he had gotten from this very hole had given him came flowing back. Getting on top of Daniel, Tom took a hold of his dick and guided it into the butt hole. It felt tight and delicious although he could not help but feel a tinge of guilt at having fucked Shania just yesterday. He drove his cock deep into Daniel's ass hole, his balls slapping against Danny's balls. Tom then began driving his dick in and out of the butt hole, each stroke harder and faster than the last. The heat within his body increased, and the whole room smelled of male sex both from them and from the couple on the next bed. Within no time, Tom felt his dick stiffening within Danny's ass hole as he shot his load of jism into him. He was filled with both a sense of satisfaction and guilt, would this hint come to haunt him one day?

CLOSURE

CHAPTER 37

Shania stood perched at the top of the hill watching her Tom and Danny riding their horses down to the river, where she hoped they would opt to take a swim, and preferably naked. She could still remember the way that Tom's cock had felt inside her pussy as it broke her virginity a couple of weeks ago. That was something that she was never going to get out of her mind, and she knew that she had to device some sort of way to make him hers completely. Horny was an understatement of how she felt whenever she remembered the day in the barn when she had found Tom masturbating and gone ahead to seduce him into making sweet love to her, love that she wanted again. Shania felt the sensitive spot in between her thighs growing moist when she thought of how Tom's dick had filled her, tearing past her hymen painfully before giving her the best experience of her life. She knew that he would probably never be hers, but neither would she let him have any other woman, even if it meant using whatever means that she had to scare the other woman away.

Shania got off her stallion and pulled out her binoculars and took them to her eyes, adjusting the focus as she looked at Tom and Daniel getting off their horses and leading them to the stream. She had the feeling that there was something more than met the eyes between the two men, and she intended to find out. She had been following them around the ranch for weeks now whenever they were alone, but she had never noticed anything odd happening between them. Daniel had healed considerably and had even stopped using the wheelchair, and of late, he had even taken back to riding his horse, although with a lot of difficulty and a little too much concern from Tom, concern that sparked off a curiosity within her since it sort of justified the rumors that had been going around that the two were gay, and probably lover's.

The thought of Tom and Daniel being gay lovers sort of got her excited in an odd way. Gay men were considered hot cakes amongst the women, and surely, she probably had the biggest weakness for them. She wondered how they made love together, and even wondered how it would feel making love with them, their forbidden cocks in her mouth and other sensitive holes in her body. That was probably every woman's dream, and to top the cream, it would be a white cock and a black cock. Black men were rumored to be very well endowed and although she had never at first considered being pounded by a black cock, the thought that Tom was probably being pounded by one got her all hot and steamy.

"Oh my God," she said under her breath as she looked at the men removing their clothes by the river after tethering their horses. "I think today is going to be my lucky day."

Her blood rushed through her body, her sex becoming liquid with desire as she watched Tom helping Danny out of his clothes. He first helped Danny out of his shirt and then pants, and Shania breathed in tightly when she noted the huge erection in his boxers. 'How could a human being have a cock so thick and long?' she wondered to herself as she tried to imagine how such a monster manhood would feel inside her cunt. Shania realized that she was just as attracted to Danny as she was to Tom, and especially now after seeing the sort of goods that he carried around in his pants. If her Tom was getting a piece of that cake, she wanted it too, and now that she had seen his cock, she wanted a piece of it. She wanted to feel it deep inside her horny folds, and she even wondered if it would feel like Tom's had. Her heart skipped a beat when Tom pulled his dark skinned lover into his arms, and their lips went together, fusing as the two men began kissing fiercely. It was the most erotic thing that Shania had ever seen, even more erotic than the sight of Tom masturbating in the barn had been.

Tom moved his hand over Daniel's muscular body and his hand finally disappeared into Danny's pants as he began rubbing it over the monster cock that was as hard as a rock. Without thinking twice, Shania instinctively pushed her hand into the waist of her pants and into her thong, pushing it in between her thighs, a finger slipping into her wet, horny slit and beginning to rub over her clit in circular delicious motions that reminded her yet again that she was no longer the innocent virgin that she had been just a few weeks ago. The two men kissed like two lovers who had known each other a long time, and Shania found herself wondering for how long the two had been lovers. Tom them moved his mouth off Daniel's and began kissing him down the neck, his hand never moving out of Danny's boxers. Tom kissed him over the chest, taking one dark nipple after the other into his mouth and sucking on it like it was the most delicious thing in the world. The picture made Shania wonder how Tom's lips would feel around her own brown nipples, sucking on them, and how her red lipstick colored lips would feel wrapped around Daniel's tiny dark nipples as she sucked on them.

Shania unbuckled her belt and pulled open her pants, before shimmying them down her fleshy thighs to her boots. She then went ahead and pulled them off her boots, and as she tossed them onto the ground, she went to the saddle of her horse and pulled her velvety best friend out of the bag, her vibrator. She had become fond of it and had bought it soon after Tom had taken her virginity and introduced her to the erotic world of sexual pleasure. It had been the only way that she could prevent herself from chasing after other men since the only man that she believed was meant for her was Tom, and now his lover too. She wanted to share them together, making love with both of them at the same time. She set a mat on the ground and then removed her soaked thong before sitting down on the mat and parting her thighs wide open to reveal her seething sex. As she turned on the vibrator and pushed the spinning head into her pussy lips, driving the vibrator deep into her vagina, she used the free hand to bring the binoculars back to her eyes.

Tom crouched infront of Daniel, kissing him down his belly. Hooking his fingers into Daniel's boxers, Tom tugged them down and Shania actually groaned when she saw the actual size of Daniel's dick. That was no ordinary cock, that was one hell of a monster cock, nice thick and shapely, with the dark circumcised head looking like it was ready to get a good sucking. As Tom's white lips curled around the dark thickness of the monster cock, Shania wondered how it would feel and taste in her mouth, and she even found her mouth watering. Tom sucked on the cock head with such professionalism as if he had been sucking on the cock his whole life. As he sucked on the dick, he wrapped his fingers around the base of the cock and began jerking the cock up and down slowly, and Shania watched in fascination as Daniel's balls tightened in their sac. How she wished that it was she who was pleasuring the black monster cock, and she found herself moving the vibrator in and out of her cunt violently. Her vagina was soggy and her love juices smeared over the vibrator and her fingers as she pleasured herself.

Tom finally pulled his mouth off the cock and stood up, kissing Danny briefly deep in the mouth, before beginning to remove his own clothes. Renewed arousal coursed through Shania's body when she saw him naked, the cock that she could remember so well as if it had just made love to her as hard as it had been the day when he took her to cloud nine. As soon as Tom was naked, Danny got onto his knees before him, and Shania watched as Danny's full dark lips wrapped around the pink head of Tom's dick, swallowing it whole and beginning to suck on it in a way that made Shania imagine that it was her clit being sucked on. She was trembling as she ran the vibrator over her throbbing clit, letting it buzz and rotate over the bud pleasurably. Danny took the whole length of the white cock as Shania looked on in consternation, surprised that Danny was taking the huge pecker deep into his mouth so comfortably.

Tom suddenly pulled Danny's head off his dick and then got onto his hands and knees like a dog. Daniel did not get up, but instead moved behind Tom and then parted his butt cheeks wide apart. Shania watched as Daniel lowered his head in between Tom's butt crack and began running his tongue up and down the length of the ass crack repeatedly, before finally bringing it to a stop on Tom's pink butt hole. Shania swallowed hard when she saw Danny stick out his tongue and push it into the rim of the butt hole, licking it like it was the sweetest Candy in the world. Danny then pulled his tongue away from the butt hole and then pushed his dark thick finger into the butt hole, driving it all the way into the hole. Shania was sweating with desire as she watched Danny move the finger in and out of the butt hole. As he finger fucked Tom's butt with one hand, the other hand went around Tom and Daniel wrapped his fingers around Tom's white dick. He began jerking the manhood in the same motions that he was finger fucking Tom, and Shania could tell the sorts of sensations that Tom was feeling just looking at his face.

Without taking his fingers away from Tom's cock, Daniel pulled his finger out of the butt hole and then took a hold of his shaft, guiding the tip into Daniel's butt hole. Daniel pushed his dark monster forward, and Shania watched as the dark length disappeared into Tom's ass. How could such a huge cock actually fit inside an ass hole, if it was a well-seasoned pussy instead, Shania could understand, or was she the one who was still very naïve when it came to matters sex? She realized that she was fucking herself in the same motions that Daniel ass fucking Tom and also jerking Tom's white snake. The intensity of their love making was so intense, Shania felt as if she was actually there with them, also taking part in the fun. She felt the heat within her horny folds beginning to rise and she quickened the pace of the dildo in and out of her vagina.

She made sure to apply pressure on her clit as the pleasure that she was feeling heightened. She tried to imagine the sort of pleasure that Tom and Daniel were feeling and she was rewarded when she saw Tom lifting his head and looking like he was screaming. And then it caught her eye, his dick erupted with cum like lava flowing out of a volcano, smearing over Daniel's fingers as it shot to the ground. Just then Daniel pushed his dick deep into Tom's butt, and Shania could tell that he was also coming. She felt a knot forming in her belly and her cunt contracted over the vibrator as she jumped over the Cliff, climaxing hard. Never in her life had she felt herself getting such a huge climax in her life before, and now more than ever, Shania knew that she had an attachment with both Daniel and Tom, an attachment that would never be shared between other people.

As she put away the vibrator, watching the men running into the river, Shania made a mental note to figure out some way to become a part of both of the men's life, even though there seemed pretty much no options. Except for the fact that she had something that she could use to blackmail Tom, a video of them making love the day that he broke her virginity. She however did not intend to use that, since it would make her feel sort of evil. The more she thought about it, a plan formulated in her mind. Tom was a very sought after man, and any of the women around town would die to have a piece of him, even if it was mere gossip. She knew what she had to do to get the men's attention, and God willing, it was going to work, and in a positive way.

The plan continued to formulate in her mind as she gathered her things and got dressed, before getting onto her horse and looking at the men one more time through the binoculars. She rode off in their direction, eager to surprise them and make it look like she had stumbled upon them by mistake while touring the prairies.

CHAPTER 38

The sun was hot and the water of the stream felt good on his back and especially after such a glorious climax. Tom Langley Sharpe III had his life exactly where he wanted it to be, and he was sure where his parents would have wanted it to be. Daniel had recovered fully and could now walk, and the ranch was doing better than ever. His love life was also going better than he had ever expected and he could not have asked for anything better. He still had some guilty feelings about making out with Shania in the barn on the day that he had arrived back from hospital, but he tried his best to put it at the back of his mind. He could not deny it though, that he'd had an extremely good time with her, one that he was not likely to forget very soon and at times he even wondered if he should go on a romp with her again. If ever he were to get married to a woman, it would be her, even though he could not imagine a life without Daniel in his life.

They swam around in the river, splashing water over themselves for a while before they finally got out of the river. Tom spread out a towel on the bank of the river and they laid on it, letting the sun dry them off. Tom was not sure for how long they had been lying there naked, and he had even began to doze off when he heard the hooves of a horse approaching them. At first he ignored it, but when he raised his head and looked in the direction of the sound, he saw Shania riding up to them completely oblivious of the fact that they were there. He looked over at Daniel, who had dozed off and had a huge hard on, probably due to the heat from the sun. There was no time for him to go for their clothes, and so he slowly got back onto his back, hoping that she would not spot them, although he knew that she would definitely spot their horses tethered a few meters away. Being naked with Daniel by the river, he suddenly felt so vulnerable, although he could not deny the sudden rush of excitement that ran through his body, even making his cock stifle with excitement. He felt his heart beat increasing with each beat of the hooves, and suddenly, Tom felt a nervous wreck. He closed his eyes, pretending to be asleep when he heard the horse coming to a stop. He listened as Shania got off the horse, and he would have liked to see the look on her face when she saw their naked bodies.

"I can't believe this, you guys actually came for a skinny dip without me," he heard her saying, and when he opened his eyes slightly, he spotted her gloating over Danny's erection almost as if she could not believe that it was real. "But I'm glad that I caught you before you left."

He heard a shuffling of clothes, and when he peered in her direction, she was removing her clothes, unbuttoning her blouse. He felt his cock stirring to life again, and especially when he remembered the way that it had felt the day when he had popped her Cherry in the barn. She peeled off her blouse and then worked off her pants and boots, before running into the water and beginning to splash about as if it was the most normal thing. Tom felt as if his dick was going to explode as it hardened even more, the heat within his balls heightening. Two naked men and one naked woman in the middle of nowhere with the sun shining warmly over their bodies, how much sexier could it get? He arched his eyes towards the water and there was one of the sexiest sights that a man could lay his eyes on. Shania's hair and body was wet, and her breasts were bobbing over the surface of the water deliciously in a way that made him want to ran into the water and squeeze them. Adding to the eroticness of the situation was the fact that she acted as if he and Danny were not there, and yet she was well aware of their hard cocks and the delicious damage that they could do to her.

CHAPTER 39

Danny awoke to the sounds of splashing water and wondered why Tom had gone back into the water without waking him up. The sun felt good against his body and the effects were evident from the heat that he felt in his loins. God, he needed another shag before they headed back to the ranch house for the afternoon. His eyes fluttered open and he sat up on his elbows, surprised to see Tom lying next to him. His eyes shot quickly to the water and there was Shania, the hot blonde that men were always chasing after unsuccessfully, naked and playing around in the water as if they did not exist. He had to admit that she looked even hotter and sexier than she did with her clothes on when she was naked and wet. A million and one questions ran through his mind as he studied her naked body, thinking for the first time in his life just how sexy she looked. She had nice firm breasts with huge brown nipples that seemed to be calling out to him to suck on them, and he wished he could see the lower half of her body that was submerged under the water. He swallowed hard as she dived under the water and disappeared for a few moments, emerging on their side of the bank and looking at him before he had the time to look away.

"Danny, finally someone is awake, I was starting to get bored, come on and swim with me, please," she said, playfully splashing water on him as he tried to quickly cover his hard on with his hands. "No need to do that, I already took a good look at it, and I must say, you have quite a package there, one that any woman would die for."

"Sh-Shania, what are you doing here, and what time did you get here?" he could not hide his curiosity as she waded out of the water, her whole body now visible to him, including her clean shaved mound that looked like it could use a pounding.

"Well, as you can see, I am here for a dip, I love swimming here, and I got here barely five minutes ago," she said, shaking her hair and running her fingers through it as she walked up to them and reached for his hands, pulling him standing as she studied his body, practically making love to him with her eyes, very tempting. "Come on and swim with me, or are you afraid of naked women, or what your friend here might think when he wakes up. Don't worry about him, he is the most precious man, and I know that he will understand, we are just having a little fun, right?"

"Well, yeah, okay, but just for a few minutes because we really have to get going, I don't know what people would think if they found the thereof us naked here," he said, cursing the burning desire within him.

He checked out her ass and her alluring figure as he followed her back into the water. He had never considered being with a woman, or making love to one, but seeing Shania here with him brought out a sort of lust that he did not know he had, the sort that he only felt for Tom. What if this was some sort of sign, because it was right in this stream that he had first become an item with Tom, and now both Shania and Tom were here. Danny freaked out when he realized that he was attracted to both Tom and Shania in a very strange way that made him want both of them.

"Do you like it, you know, my ass, because I bet you are staring at it?" she asked, the question throwing him completely off guard.

"What?" he couldn't think of anything else to say.

"My buttocks, silly, I know that you are staring at them," she said as they waded deeper into the water, before she stopped before him and turned around to look at him, her white breasts practically touching his chest, and igniting a flame within him, a flame that he was not sure he would be able to control.

"Well, yeah, you have a very good figure and a nice ass," he said to her, his heart skipping a beat when he noted the heat in her hazel eyes.

"Really, how about you touch them and squeeze them, huh, I'm feeling kind of naughty and generous today," she said, moving closer to him, her breasts pressing against his chest as his erection dug into her belly.

"Shania, I-I don't think this is really a good idea," Daniel said even though his body thought otherwise and he wanted to do the dirtiest things to her.

"Stop kidding yourself, Daniel, let go of your inhibitions for once and enjoy what you have before you, while you still have it," she said, placing her hands around his neck and pulling him closer to her.

How in the world could he resist anything so sexy? He looked down into her eyes and then lower to her lips. She licked her lower lip deliciously and it was almost irresistible for him not to kiss her. He found his head lowering to hers, his dark lips seeking hers as they began kissing passionately, almost hungrily. Daniel surrendered to her demands and she parted her lips slightly for the sweet invasion of his tongue into her mouth as their tongues began dancing erotically together. His hands automatically went down to her breasts and he began massaging the mounds, taking her nipples in between his fingers and rolling them around in semi circles as they pebbled with arousal. Shania moved her hand down his back, squeezing his tight ass before reaching in between them and wrapping her fingers around his thickness. He loved the way that her body responded, because he could feel her shaking as she began to jerk his dick up and down slowly.

CHAPTER 40

The mere feel of the enormous cock was enough to set her whole body on fire despite the fact that they were in the water waist deep. Shania had never imagined that a man could have such a huge dick, and she was not only touching it, but she intended it to be the second and only other cock to fuck her. Daniel knew how to kiss, and she felt as if he was making love to her with his mouth. The heat in between her thighs was blazing, and she had creamed up in ways that she had only ever done for Tom. As they made out in the river, Shania realized that she was in love with both men. One of his hands moved off her breast and began moving down her belly, disappearing in between her thighs as she parted them to give him better access to her goodies. She moaned into his mouth when she felt his finger slipping into her slick folds to begin rubbing over her throbbing clit. It felt slutty being in love with two men at the same time, but Shania could not help it. She now wanted Danny just as much as she had always wanted Tom, no inhibitions to stop her. Somehow, the two men had sort of brainwashed her and made her common sense disappear.

"Danny, I have a confession to make," she said amidst the kissing. "I think I'm in love."

"In love?" he commented, temporarily moving his lips away from hers and looking her deep in the eyes as his finger moved in and out of her slit deliciously. "In love with who, Shania?"

"Is it wrong to be in love with two men at the same time?" she said as he nibbled on her earlobe deliciously, sending waves to all the erotic spots on her body.

"Being in love is not wrong at all, but you should let them know so that they can make the choice," he replied as his mouth moved over one of her nipples, his dark lips sucking the brown peak pleasantly.

"Holy fuck, that feels good," Shania said, taking her hands down to his head and pressing it harder onto her breast as he pleasured her nipple with his mouth, sucking and nibbling on it.

He took the peak in between his teeth and bit it lightly, and Shania felt a wave of pleasure going all the way to her throbbing clit. Danny definitely knew how to make love with his mouth, and if he could make her feel this good sucking on her nipple, she wondered how it would feel like if he were sucking on her clit instead. As he sucked on her nipple, he began rubbing his finger over her clit, increasing the pressure slightly to make her quiver with delight. Suddenly, he pulled his lips away from hers and then lifted her off the ground easily, carrying her out of the water.

"I wanna make love to you, Shania, I wanna fuck you like crazy and then you can tell me all about your lover's. I wish that Tom was awake so that he could join us," he said, kissing her again as they waded out of the water.

Shania could not remember having felt so aroused and needy for cock. In her mind she could already feel the huge dark cock pumping in and out of her love slit, the friction of the thickness taking her to another world. She admired his strength and wondered if he intended to make love to her with all of it. she also wondered if Tom would wake up before they were done, and if he would join them or hate them forever. She had the feeling that he would actually enjoy it, making her wonder how it would feel being boned by two men at the same time.

CHAPTER 41

Tom's blood was rushing through his veins at an alarming speed as he watched Danny carrying Shania out of the water. They definitely made a good pair, but it would be better if they were a trio instead. Both Danny and Shania were hot as hell, and he felt their heat rubbing off on him, his dick aching more than it ever had before as desire coursed through every vein in his body.

"I still can't believe that you have made me so horny, and your words are making me even hornier. I just wish that Tom was also awake so that you could both play with my body the way that you want," she said as Daniel walked up to the towel and placed her on it.

"Are you sure that you can handle the two of us at the same time?" Danny asked, standing before her as she studied his dick while sitting on the towel.

"Good question, Danny, it is such a pleasure to see you Shania," Tom said, finally breaking the silence as he sat up on his elbows, pretending that he had just woken up, and feeling hornier than he had ever felt in his life.

"Danny," Shania said, turning to look at him as her hand flew to cover her mouth, shock registering on her face. "I did not know that you were awake."

"Well, honey, I'm wide awake and ready to take you up on the offer of a threesome, I just hope that you are ready and will be able to satisfy the both of us," Tom said, getting up and parting her thighs before lowering his head in between her thighs and sniffing it in.

Tom parted her thighs a little wider and then moved his head lower, his mouth aiming for her pussy. His tongue parted her vagina lips and slipped in, giving him a taste of her nectar. Her arousal was evident by the wetness of her cunt, and as he sucked her clit into his lips, Shania moaned.

"Ohh, Tom, ssss," she moaned, taking her hands down to his head and pressing his head harder into her crotch, smearing his face with her love juices.

As Tom started lapping at her cunt, Danny moved next to her, standing with his dick right next to her head. Shania turned to look at the black monster cock and wrapped her fingers around the base of the thickness, her lips moving slowly towards the head, before curling around it as she began to suck on it. Arching his eyes to look at her, Tom saw Shania taking more and more of the manhood into her mouth. The contrast of her white lips curved over Danny's chocolate colored dick was the most arousing thing at that moment, and it made his own dick ach for attention. Tom drove his finger into her cunt as he sucked on her clit, pushing it all the way into her wet, slick folds and then hooking the digits as he pulled the finger out, a technique that he had once read makes the finger touch the most sensitive spot in a woman's cunt, her G spot.

"Mmhh," she groaned onto the cock in her mouth, confirming what he had read.

He sucked on her clit hard as he pumped his finger in and out of her soggy cunt, hooking it each time that he pulled out and he could feel her trembling everytime that he did that. Her cunt became even more liquid with each stroke, and that got Tom more and more aroused. Within no time, he knew that he needed to be inside her, he needed to get a feel of her pussy again, after all, she was his, he is the one who had taken her virginity, just like he had Danny's. He pulled his soggy head out of her cunt and looked up at the way she was blowing Danny's dick, a glorious look on Danny's face. He stood up and kissed Danny full in the lips, giving him a taste of Shania's love juices as Danny's tongue slipped into his mouth. Tom felt Shania's lips wrapping around the head of his shaft as she began sucking on it, playing her tongue over the tip and spreading his precum deliciously over the sensitive skin. Tom groaned into Danny's mouth as pleasure coursed through his body, the need to bone her now stronger than ever. He finally pulled his lips away from Danny's.

"I need to be inside her right now, I can't wait a moment longer," Tom said to Danny, who nodded understandingly although Tom could see in his eyes that he too was in desperate need of a romp. "Come on, Shania, are you ready?"

"As ready for you as the day that you broke my virginity," she said, getting up and then getting onto her hands and knees, her head facing Daniel.

She took a hold of Daniel's cock and moved her head closer to it, her lips enveloping Danny's dark cock as she began sucking on it. Tom moved behind Shania and got onto his knees, parting her butt cheeks and running his tongue through the butt crack. He pressed a finger into the rim of her butt hole, and she moaned out in pleasure as he drove it all the way into her butt. With his other hand, he took a hold of his dick and guided it in between her thighs, easing the tip into her vagina. She was slick and wet as he drove the cock all the way into her love nest, loving the feel of her wet tightness on his dick. Gripping her by the hips, Tom began moving his dick in and out of her pussy, the friction between the two organs bringing him immense pleasure, pleasure that he was not sure he would ever be able to get tired of. His balls slammed against her pussy lips whenever he pushed his pecker in, and he could feel the length of his dick rubbing over her clit on every stroke. He spanked her buttock with one hand as he shagged her harder and faster, and the heat being generated by the contact of his cock and her vagina heightened.

There was a burning sensation in his balls and he knew that it was his seed preparing to shoot into her vagina. Her pussy suddenly tightened over the cock and Tom knew that Shania was coming, her cunt creaming up even more. The sliminess of her juices over his dick brought him such intense pleasure, Tom could not hold it back any more. Parting her butt cheeks, he drove a finger into her butt hole, pushing it deep as he also drove his dick deep into her folds. His cum erupted into her cunt like a volatile volcano as his pleasure reached its peak. He felt the pleasure rippling through his body right down to the nerve endings of his toes.

CHAPTER 42

Shania gripped her cunt muscles over the cock pounding her tightly, heightening the level of her climax as Tom's semen shot into her vagina. She had been longing to get this feeling of being so filled up again since the last time that Tom had made love to her, and she felt as if she had died and gone to heaven. As she sucked on the huge dark cock in her mouth, Shania realized that her pleasure had been so intense, she was actually holding her breath, a cold sweat breaking off on her forehead. All of the nerves in her body felt alive, alive in the most exciting way and to imagine that there was still yet another cock waiting to pound her. She felt like a slut, her hunger for sex reaching peaks she had never imagined existed, but she did not care. What mattered was that she was with the two men that she was attracted to the most, and they were gladly sharing her despite the fact that they were more gay oriented. The feel of Tom's finger wiggling about inside her ass hole and rubbing over his dick through the thin membrane that separated her two holes was the apex of her pleasure.

"Oh my God, that is the biggest climax of my life," she breathed heavily as Tom finally pulled his softening cock out of her cunt. "It brought back such a pleasurable memory that I have never been able to get out of my mind. It feels so thrilling that I still have yet another cock to deal with."

She stood up and pulled Daniel into her arms, her lips fusing over his as she kissed him deeply and urgently. She could still fell the tremors from the orgasm she'd just had still rippling through her body, and it made her wonder what sort of climax she would get with Danny's dark snake buried deep inside her. Danny finally pulled away from her and got onto his hands and knees on the towel, his head going down to Tom's smeary cock. As he licked away the mess of their love juices from Tom's dick, Shania made Tom to lie down and then got on top of him, straddling his head and lowering her dripping cunt to his mouth so that he could get a taste of the delicious cocktail of love juices inside her vagina. Tom wrapped his hands around her thighs, pulling her down onto him and beginning to lap at her cunt. The thought that she still had another monster cock to deal with still had her feeling very horny and excited and she trembled with pleasure. She reached her hand out to Danny, running it over his back before slipping it into his butt crack and pushing her finger all the way to his butt hole. She felt his trembling as she pushed her finger in slightly, not pushing it all the way because of her long nail. He seemed to enjoy it tremendously, moving his ass from side to side appreciatively.

Daniel sucked on Tom's cock in such a way that it began to get hard again in his mouth, and Shania marveled at the way that Tom got back from an orgasm so quickly. The white shaft was soon fully erect and she looked at the way that Danny's dark lips were moving up and down on it, feasting on it as he sucked and licked it. Her own cunt was also being pleasured beyond doubt, and within no time, all that she wanted to feel a love rod inside her, this time a black cock that would spit into her, filling up her womb the way that the white cock had just done. She rubbed her cunt over Tom's face for a moment and then got up just as Danny also got up. He pulled her into his arms, his dark lips seeking hers as they began kissing. She could taste the residue of the love juices that he had sucked off Tom's cock on his tongue, and it made her dizzy with excitement.

Shania wrapped her hands around his shoulders and hoisted herself up, their lips never disengaging. She wrapped her legs around his waist and could feel his cock at the entrance of her pussy. He held her by the hips, supporting her as she lowered herself onto him, his dark thickness disappearing into her hot slick folds pleasurably. He felt thick, hard and addictive as he started moving his dick in and out of her cunt. The heat from the sun heightened the desire that she felt as he fucked her, and she could feel his thickness moving her clit in and out as he drilled her. Shania felt Tom moving behind her, and before she knew it, he parted her butt cheeks and the tip of his cock pierced her butt hole. She held her breath, not sure if she was going to be able to handle two cocks at the same time, and not just ordinary cocks, but monster rods that would make another woman green with envy. She was sandwiched between the two men she loved, one dark skinned and the other white skinned, and the thought heightened her erotic desires in such a way that she did not even want to imagine how intense her orgasm was going to be.

Tom inched his dick into her butt slowly by slowly, stopping every now and then to let her butt hole adjust to the new intrusion. It felt a little uncomfortable at first, but the moment that he began moving his dick in and out of her butt, Shania knew that it was something she would always lust after. The men fucked her in such a way that when one cock was pushing in, the other was pulling out, and Shania had never imagined that she would ever be this filled up with cock. It was pleasant and highly fulfilling as she let both men plough her love holes pleasurably. Something about the way that they were making love to her so intensely gave her the feeling that this was all just the beginning of something special, something special between all three of them.

She felt the heat within her folds heightening as the men pounded her harder and faster, her ass and pussy getting bonked to the maximum. She could feel every inch of each cock as they moved in and out of the vagina and butt hole and they felt glorious. Her clit felt like it was in heaven as the huge dark monster cock worked its way deliciously over it, and it was not long before she felt her orgasm sparking to life. Her cunt contracted over the cock within it, gripping it tightly as she exploded hard into a climax that made her dizzy with pleasure. Almost as if on cue, she felt the cock in her ass shooting a hot load of cum into her bum and as she was still reeling in the pleasure of being ass filled with semen, she felt Danny's dick stiffening within her as he pushed it as deep as it could go, just before a very huge load of semen flooded into her vagina.

Three glorious orgasms rocked within her at the same time, something that was way beyond any woman's expectations, and if ever she was going to gossip about it with her girlfriends, they were going to be a jealous lot. She could almost picture the looks on their faces when she told them that she had been sandwiched and fucked by two monster cocks, one black and the other white, almost unbelievable. There was also the fact that she was madly in love with both men, and right now more than ever, there was no way that she would ever be able to get them out of her system even if she tried hard.

CHAPTER 43

The ride back to the ranch house was rather quiet. Danny was fighting with the mixed emotions in his mind. After the experience with Shania and Tom by the river, he felt as if he was in love with both of them, as if they all shared something special, a special kind of bond that . The three of them rode in the direction of the ranch house and Danny took the hind, studying both Tom and Shania as they rode silently.

"Hey, Shania, there is something that you promised to tell me," he said, suddenly remembering something that she had told him while his mind had been foggy with desire.

"What was that, honey, I seem to have forgotten, and I sure hope that I was not too high to have blubbered without thinking?" she turned to look back at him, winking as a smile lit up on her face.

"You said something about being in love and then said that you would tell me about it, after…. You know," he galloped to catch up with them, eager to know who the person she was in love with was.

"Oh that, did I really say that?" she asked, a deep blush forming on her lips as they colored.

"Hey, quit beating around the bush and tell us about it, who is this lucky dude?" Tom asked, turning to look at her.

"Okay, right, so I'm I love, what does it matter to you guys," she said, Danny noting the blush on her face again.

"Hell yeah, it matters a whole deal, I mean, we just had the most mind blowing sex just a while ago," Tom said.

"Hmm, so it looks like you really enjoyed it, huh, tell you guys what, come camping with me in the hills as I check out the cattle on our ranch and I'll tell you all about it around the bonfire, if we do get a chance to talk, that is, because I know that you are two extremely hot dudes who might not be able to keep their hands to themselves," she said after a moment of thought.

"Well, Tom, it looks like we have ourselves a very secretive woman here, but the camping idea is a pretty good one, since we were also planning to head to the far end of the ranch sometime this week," Danny said, picturing a camping trip with just the three of them and all of the dangerously delicious things that they could do together.

"Yeah, that is right, when were you planning on going for the camping trip on your ranch," Tom said, and Danny could tell that he too liked the idea.

"I really don't know, the idea just popped up in my mind now, but we can go as soon as you are ready. When do you think we will go for the trip?" she asked.

"I really don't know, maybe we can make a decision once we have spoken to Valerie. We need to know the key points of the ranch to go to," Tom replied, and Danny couldn't help but feel that intense feeling of excitement coursing through him.

"And that means that you are coming with us to the house, hoping that Valerie is back from the city," Daniel added.

"Sounds like a plan, and I sure hope that we will be alone so that we can pick up where we left off," she said.

"I never knew that you were this randy, I only assumed that you were just very smitten over me," Tom smiled at her.

"Is that what you think I am, smitten over you?" she smiled. "If that is the case, then you still have quite a lot of learning to do when it comes to knowing women."

"And why do you say that, because I also think that Tom is right," Danny wondered aloud, still trying to ponder who she was in love with, probably Tom, but she had mentioned something about being in love with two people.

"Well then, my dear Danny, I think you too have quite a lot of learning to do too, when it comes to women's feelings," she said mysteriously.

CHAPTER 44

"I really wonder who Shania is in love with," Tom said to Danny on their drive to town almost a week after their hot encounter with Shania by the river.

"If it isn't you, my dear, I really don't know who it is," Danny smiled at him as Tom lay back on the passenger seat of the truck.

"Yeah, me too, can you imagine that she saved her virginity for me and then cornered me when she found me masturbating in the barn the day I came back from hospital," Tom said, revealing something that he had kept from his lover for weeks. "I'm sorry, I had meant to tell you about it sooner."

"Don't sweat about it, Tom, I think I actually like her myself, and she is one hell of a good lover. Heck, I would not mind making love to her again if I got the chance," Danny said as the car sped away from a traffic light the minute it turned green.

"I think she is a really dynamic woman. Taking the both of us at the same time and not flinching about it, not very many women can manage that. I actually can't wait until tomorrow when we go camping, I'm pretty sure that it is going to be very interesting indeed," Tom said, his dick stifling in his pants when he thought of the wonderful things that they could do as a trio during the camping trip.

"You had better stop thinking about sex and think about the derby, this is your first race since your victory months ago and I need for you to really concentrate," Danny said, bringing Tom's mind back to the present.

His mind went back to the derby in which he was participating in as a jockey with his horse, Eagle. He had been practicing quite a lot lately with Valerie training him and even though he felt in tip top form, he was still a little nervous about it all. The accident that had happened at the last race still sent shivers down his spine, and he could still picture Danny being pushed off his speeding horse by the red head as if it was yesterday. It was a good thing that the red head had been put away for a very long time, and most especially because the chief of police was a horse riding fan and had been there when the incident had occurred.

"You look tense, are you okay?" Danny glanced over at him.

"Yeah, I'm fine, I was just remembering the dreadful events that happened the last time, it is a good thing that the racist red head was locked up for a very long time," Tom said, his muscles relaxing a little.

"I hate thinking about it, it was like a nightmare to me, something that I will not be forgetting very soon," Danny said. "Well, let us think of the good times ahead of us, living in the past is not going to show us the way forward."

The racecourse was packed with visitors and participators, and as would have it, most of the bets this time were on Tom although he had missed out on a number of races over the weeks as he recovered from the shock and all. Valerie had already arrived and was with the stallions from the ranch that were participating in the races.

"All set for the race?" Valerie asked as Tom walked up to Eagle and began patting him down his mane.

"Yeah, I'm ready to kick some ass today. I can see that nowadays there is a lot more security around the tracks," Tom said, feeling a lot better when he saw a lot of police officers moving around the field, including the police chief.

"It is going to be a pretty tough race today, there are some experienced jockeys who have come from Europe and I think this is going to be a real game changer. There is also a sheikh here who has also brought a number of horses from his stables, and he has put up a fortune for them. If we win these races, I think we will just have moved to another level of wealth," Valerie said, saddling up the horse as Tom double checked the horse shoes to see that they were comfortable.

"I love challenges, and even you know that, Valerie," Tom said, just as someone came behind him and soft feminine fingers covered his eyes in a way suggesting that he guess who it was, and from the perfume, he knew instantly that it was Shania.

"Shania, is that you, because I can recognize that perfume from a mile away," he said, feeling a wave of excitement at knowing that she was also here to support him, and for some reason, that being very important to him.

Maybe it was because of the passion that they had shared recently or maybe it was because of something much stronger that he felt but could not understand. As she opened his eyes, he turned around slowly, and there she was standing in a nice pair of Jean's that hugged her body in a sexy way, disappearing into a pair of brown riding boots. Danny was standing beside her, a huge grin on his face, while Valerie looked at them with eyes that questioned what was happening.

"I didn't know that you knew me that well," she said kissing him lightly on the lips as she hugged him.

"You've been chasing after me for years, how could I not know you so well, and in all aspects, if you know what I mean," he said, winking at her.

"Well, I just came around hoping that I will be your good luck charm during the races," she smiled sweetly at him as he pulled on his riding cap.

"Thank you, Shania, it means quite a lot to me," he said, looking at the way that her breasts were heaving up and down in her blouse in a sexy way.

It was an entertaining time at the races, and Tom emerged the winner in most of the races that he participated in. There was much stiffer and experienced competition and Tom was Glad that Eagle had turned out to be one of the best stallions on this side of the continent. He easily out did the more experienced horses giving their owners a run for their money. Bets were placed and most of those that had their bets on Eagle went smiling all the way to the bank.

"Now that is what I call professional racing," Danny ran up to him as he brought his horse to a stop after winning the final race of the day.

"Yeah, it was an adrenaline filled day, I have never felt such a rush, I almost felt as if I was high on cock or something," Tom said, getting off the horse just as a group of journalists ran over to him.

Not used to this kind of publicity, he answered their questions politely grinning at the cameras until his jaws hurt. He was glad when Valerie came to his rescue, the Frenchman quickly whisking him away to the safety of the private rooms.

"Quite a lot of drama going on out there, you are now the talk of the town," Valerie said as he led him towards the changing rooms so that he could change into something appropriate to wear for the after party that had been organized by the event organizers.

"I don't think that I'll ever get used to this kind of publicity, I would rather my quiet life that I have always lived," Tom said, even though he knew that it was going to be very hard to live a quiet life and wondering how he was going to survive with the paparazzi always on his tail, looking for the slightest details of his life.

"Tom, can I ask you a question?" Valerie asked, surprising Tom with the curious tone of his voice. "And I need for you to answer me very honestly."

"Hey, Valerie, you are like a father to me and we have shared many secrets, what would you like to know?" Tom turned to look at the older man that he had grown so fond of from an early age.

"I don't know how to put this, is there something that I do not know about happening between you, Danny and Shania? I'm sorry, it is just that she acted very, strange, when she was with you earlier on, and I saw you return that look," Valerie asked, catching Tom completely off guard since he had intended to find a way of letting him know what was happening at some point, but not like this.

"Come on, Valerie, what makes you think that there is something going on between us?" Tom asked, deciding that he was not yet ready to explain the details right now, and besides, he could not quite understand what was going on in his heart.

"Tom, I have known you and Danny since you were children, and believe me, I know how to read your eyes. I think you two are both in love with Shania, you are involved in some sort of love triangle," okay, the cat was out of the bag, making Tom feel as if his legs would give in. "And what is more, I think you have already become intimate with her and had sex with her, I saw the glow in her cheeks when she was with you two, first with Danny and then you."

"Wow, I don't know what to say, Valerie," Tom said after a moment of silence.

"You wanna know what I think about it? I think that it is a good thing, and it came right in the Nick of time. Right now you are going to be very famous on the track and having a woman around is good for your image. It is good to keep people guessing about your sexuality," Valerie said, the statement completely surprising Tom since he had thought that he would begin giving him all that one partner kind of shit.

"Are you kidding me?" he asked.

"No, think about it, it is good to keep people guessing as to whether you are gay, bi or straight, and besides, Shania is a one of a kind type of woman, hot, sexy and intelligent, things that it is very difficult to find in one woman. I saw the intense heat in your eyes when you looked at her, it was the same heat that comes into your eyes when you are with Danny. I say go for it, boy, don't treat it as just a fling, go the whole nine yards. One day you and Danny might want to have kids and what better than to have kids with her, I'm growing old and I wanna hold your kids before I die," Valerie said as Tom struggled to digest what he was saying since it was all coming in overload. "Let me let you freshen up and change, but think about it my boy, don't deny what you have."

With that, he patted Tom on the back and walked away as Tom entered the changing room, Valerie's words replaying over and over in his mind. He stripped out of his riding clothes and went into the shower, letting the hot water massage his body as he tried to weigh what his heart felt. Shania had been in love with him right from the time that they were in their early teens, while Tom had realized that he had some sort of feelings for her not very long ago. She sort of lit up a flame in his heart, not quite like the one Daniel did, but very similar and special in its own way. Could it be that he was in love with both Daniel and Shania? The thought confused Tom because he had always had some sort of gay thing since he was a child. He also wondered if Valerie had been right in his thoughts on Danny.

What if Danny was also in love with Shania, could such a relationship ever work out, could the three of them be lovers and probably partners for life? There were so many 'what's' going on through his mind as he soaped up his body and began to clean himself. By the time that he came out of the shower he was more confused than ever and did not know what to do about the situation. The best thing would be to let things work themselves out, and if they were all to become an item, it would come naturally to them. There was something that Valerie had said that was right, though, it would be a good idea to keep his fans guessing his sexuality. The intrigue over his sexual affiliation would definitely make the headlines of magazines since every journalist would want to get to the bottom of it.

CHAPTER 45

Valerie had changed into an evening gown that hugged her body in a sexy way, showing off all of her curves as it went right down to her ankles. Right through the center of the front was a slit that came right up stopping short of her crotch and showing off her sexy thighs. All the eyes in the ballroom turned to look at her as she sauntered in, her hair tied in a bum on the top of her head. She had a reason to be dressed like this, she had the lovers of her life to meet and impress. Men looked at her longingly, and she could even see some of them practically undressing her with their eyes as she stood rooted on the spot scanning the room for where her two men were. A tall lanky dude dressed in a black tux approached her, eyeing her as he would have loved to have sex with her right there.

"Hello, beautiful, care for some company?" he said, swirling the champagne in his glass.

"I'm sorry, handsome, some other time, I'm booked right now," she said as she spotted one of her girlfriends walking into the room. "Diana, here."

She hurried over to Diana before the surprised dude could utter another word and hugged her warmly.

"I wasn't expecting to see you here," she said to her friend as she pulled away from her, holding her at an arm's length away as her friend checked her out.

"You look stunningly sexy, Shania, you have to show me where you bought this dress," she said as Shania moved around in a circle to give her friend a good look at the outfit.

"Thanks, Diana, what brings you to this party, I thought that you considered them very boring?" she asked, looking at her friend with curiosity written all over her face.

"What do you mean what brings me here, how could I miss out the chance to see the guys that you talked so highly about?" her friend said in a low voice. "And besides, there seem to be very many hot dudes in here, who knows what could happen!"

"I still think that you are one of the craziest women that I know, what if Eddie finds out that you are here?" Shania asked, referring to her husband.

"Nah, no way he is finding out, he flew to New York on a business trip and won't be back in a week," she smiled, showing off her fingers to show Shania that she was not wearing a ring and intended to have a no strings attached sexual engagement during that time.

"I can't believe you, a cheating wife now?" Shania said as they moved around the ballroom, her eyes peeled out for Tom or Danny.

They moved up to a tale with cocktails and got themselves each a drink, before heading off to see if they could find seats that were vacant. It looked like her men were not yet in the house, and hoped that they would be in attendance, since this was meant to be a surprise, her being there.

"There are so many hot guys In here I can already feel myself getting all hot and excited down there," Diana said, flirtingly at a guy who was passing by their seat, her long fake lashes making her look sexy.

"I didn't know that married women could get so horny," Shania said as Diana curled her long legs, beautiful thighs peeping out of the short dress that she wore, dressed for the kill.

"Believe me, it comes to a point when one craves variety, and especially after listening to your story of being boned by two huge cocks at the same time."

"Lower your voice, silly, I don't want the whole world thinking that I'm a slut when I'm not. I think I am bloody in love with both men and I just don't know what to do about it," Shania said, sipping on her champagne.

"If I was in your shoes, I would tell them exactly what I feel, tell them that you are in love with both of them and that you would like to have a relationship with both of them. Time waits for no man, and the sooner the better, you never know, they might just feel the same way about you, and damn, I will envy your situation if they do. Imagine having two willing cocks to play around with, forbidden cocks that belong in the gay world, girlfriend, you are the luckiest woman in the world," Diana said, getting up and heading for another drink as Shania contemplated what her friend had just told her.

Diana was right, maybe she should just go ahead and tell Tom and Daniel exactly how she felt about them, but the thing was how she would begin, since it sounded like a really crazy idea. What if she told them and it ruined the good erotic relationship that she had with them? It was all really confusing and put her in a tight spot, but she decided that she would tell them about it during the camping trip tomorrow evening. She was going to have to gather all of her guts to do it, and the best thing would probably to spill the beans after they had made sweet love to her. She trembled at the thought of feeling the two delicious cocks once again, drilling her like it was the end of the world. Diana was right, she was the luckiest woman that there was in this world.

"A sexy woman seated alone and smiling weirdly to herself, how amusing," a familiar voice said, and when she turned around, there stood Danny behind the seat looking more handsome than ever in a black tux as he stood there looking down at her, his eyes moving from her face to her cleavage before he swallowed hard. Behind him in the distance, she noticed Tom walking in with Valerie and another guy whom she recognized as one of their jockeys.

"Danny, I am so glad to see you, I was wondering what time you were going to arrive," she said, jumping up and running around the seat to throw her arms around his shoulders as she hugged him lovingly, while he kissed her on the cheek.

"What a pleasant surprise, honey, I did not think that you would be here," he said into her ear, and she was sure that she felt a slight movement in his pants against her belly, an erotic tremble sending waves through her body all the way to her cunt.

"Oh my goodness, is that you, Shania, you look... priceless!" Tom said walking over to them as she pulled away from Danny and also hugged him while he whispered in her ear. "Seeing you like this, looking so sexy is going to make me lose control over my emotions."

"I would love it if you could, maybe we could meet up in the washrooms a little later on for a quickie, huh," she whispered back and also felt his dick moving slightly in his pants. he pulled away quickly before she could feel more, and she knew that it was because the longer they hugged, the more he ran the risk of getting a hard on right here infront of everyone at the party.

"Well, well, well, girlfriend, and who are all these handsome guys? Ah, wait a minute, I think I know you, and you too," Diana said walking over to them.

Shania went ahead and did the introductions, and she noted the way that Diana immediately got comfortable with Juan, the jockey from Tom's ranch, cornering him for herself and beginning to flirt with him almost immediately. He was much younger than her, probably 17 or 18, while she was 21, but that was the way that Diana liked it. She believed that the old men were for the money, while the young men were for mind blowing sex. So much for her wild friend's philosophies, she was one hell of a wild card. Danny seemed to have floated away with Valerie to talk to another rancher from the country, and so she turned her attention to Tom.

"Well, honey, is that washroom appointment still pending, because I am feeling really itchy down there," she said, snuggling into him on the seat and resting her hand loosely on his crotch in a way that would not attract attention.

"Now that you mention it, maybe we could sneak off before there are too many guests here," he said, kissing her deeply in the mouth, before they both stood up and began heading towards the washrooms as Shania winked at Diana, who looked at her enviously.

The washrooms were at the far end of the room and by the time that they got there, Shania was hot and horny and she had turned liquid in all the right places. She could feel her moistness spreading through her thong, and she prayed that it would not spread into her dress. Since it was the ladies washrooms, Shania was the first one to enter, before Tom followed her when nobody was seeing. The moment that they were inside, he pushed her into a toilet booth and locked the door as he pulled her into his arms, his lips locking onto hers urgently as they kissed hungrily. Once again, all of her inhibition was gone the way that it always did when she was with Tom or Daniel, and she parted her thighs as she felt him pushing his hand into the slit of her dress and up her thighs to her crotch. He began rubbing his fingers over her pussy lips over the fabric of the soaked thong, and Shania felt herself trembling with desire the way that she always did when she was with him.

"I love it when you get wet like this," Tom said, moving his lips away from hers and hiking her dress up and over her hips. He hooked his fingers into her thong and tugged it off, taking it to his nose and sniffing it in as she kicked it off her feet.

He then stuffed it into the pocket of his tuxedo and then proceeded to pull his fly open, reaching into his pants for his dick and pulling it out. Shania was blazing with lust when she saw the huge manhood, and holding the cock, Tom moved towards her. He pushed her against the door of the booth and then took a hold of one of her thighs, lifting it up as he pressed himself against her. She reached down for his pennies and guided it in between her thighs, and as he pushed forward, it pierced into her love slit deliciously, the thickness making her gasp in pleasure. As Tom drove the cock into her snatch, Shania arched her waist towards him, her cunt meeting him and swallowing him in whole as he began fucking her hard and fast. She put her hands around his neck and pulled his head toward hers, kissing him deeply and passionately as they made love. She felt his dick rubbing pleasurably over her clit as it moved in and out of her cunt, and she had to will herself not to moan out in pleasure. She was in heaven, pleasure heaven, where she belonged and where she hoped to remain forever. The fact that they were having a quickie in such a risky place seemed to heighten the desire that she felt, and she quickly felt the heat within her folds starting to increase as she neared her orgasm.

"Oh, Tom, harder, harder please," she pleaded with him softly as he quickened the pace of his dick in and out of her cunt, driving it in to the hilt whenever he pushed in.

His thickness felt delicious within her folds, the friction of his dick against the horny folds of her cunt feeling next to heavenly. From the way that tome was breathing heavily, she could tell that he too was coming closer and closer to the climax of their experience. She gripped her cunt muscles over his cock, milking him whenever he pulled out and also heightening the contact between the two organs. Voices sounded outside the booth in the washrooms and then were gone almost as soon as they had come, and that is when Shania could not hold it a moment longer. She jerked her hips forward urgently as a tremor shook through her cunt, her orgasm exploding deliciously.

"Oh fuck, there it comes, Tom, I'm coming, I'm coming," she moaned as her climax rocked her magnanimously, awakening every erotic nerve within her body.

He began fucking her almost roughly as he rode her through her climax, his dick pumping like a piston in and out of her cunt.. just as her climax came to an end, Shania felt yet another orgasm glowing to life and rocking her again, although this time not as explosive as the first one. She was still reeling in pleasure when she heard Tom grunting in a low voice, just as his semen went shooting into her vagina, filling her up deliciously as if blended with her pussy juices. She milked the cock of all its glorious love juices until Tom's dick finally began to get soft and he pulled it out of her cunt.

"Thank you, honey, I really needed that," she said, letting her dress fall down. "My underwear, please."

"Sorry, princess, but I'll be holding on to them for the rest of the evening, it will be less of a hustle if we get a chance to do this again," he smiled at her, zipping up his pants as she noted the slight cum stain, evidence of the naughty thing they had just done.

With that, they sneaked out of the washroom and headed back to the ballroom with Shania hoping that nobody would notice that she was not wearing any underwear beneath her dress. It was a Friday and it looked like this was going to be one hell of a good weekend, if things had began so well for her.

CHAPTER 46

Tom drained his second mug of coffee as he went through the day's newspaper, a big hangover making his head heavy.

"So, you guys still going camping today?" Valerie asked walking ito the kitchen and hugging Sophia, the cook, warmly.

"Yeah, we will ride out after an early lunch today, I just hope that Shania does not oversleep, we had quite a lot to drink last evening at the party," Tom said, hating the fact that he could not even remember coming back home.

"Yeah, she was pretty wasted when we dropped her off," Valerie said, pouring himself some coffee, as Tom tried to jog his memory so that he could remember what had happened last night. "Juan on the other hand, took off with that randy friend of hers, what was her name again, Diana?"

"Yeah, if I'm not wrong, they did not even stay very long at the party, quite a horny woman that one," Tom said, remembering Juan and the older brunette sneaking out of the party, a huge erection in Juan's pants, and Diana barely able to keep her hands off it. They were probably at it the whole night, fucking like there was no tomorrow. "Poor fellow must be pretty drained by now."

"You bet, anyway, did you think about what I told you yesterday, you know, regarding Shania?" Tom should have guessed that was coming.

"I think I'm just going to let things fall into place naturally, if at all there is going to be anything between us, I'm sure it will all just fall into place," Tom said, his mind made up not to push, but to try.

"I guess you are right, take the weekend off, I'll take care of everything on this end until you come back, and I sure hope that you will all come back with some exciting news for me," Valerie said, as Tom got up to leave the room before Valerie pushed the topic.

"I think I had better wake Daniel up so that we can start preparing our gear. Please ask Sophia to make sure that she has our grub packed and ready by eleven," he said, walking out of the kitchen and making his way up the stairs to check on Daniel, and besides, a really cold shower would do him some good in the state that he was.

When he got to the bedroom, Daniel was still fast asleep completely fully clothed, including his shoes, and he looked so peaceful, Tom decided that he would wake him up later. He walked into the bathroom and removed his clothes, and as he reached into the pocket of his pants, he realized that he still had Shania's thong. He took it to his nose, breathing in her scent as he felt his cock shifting excitedly. Life seemed to have taken a new turn, a turn that he would never have imagined only weeks ago, because now he was in love with two people at the same time and he did not know how to deal with it. Tucking the thong back into his pocket, he tossed the pants aside and then walked into the shower, turning on the cold water and stepping under it for a sobering shower. By the time that he was done showering, Tom felt energized and as fresh as ever, all symptoms of the hangover gone, and now ready to begin with the new day. He changed into clothes and went to make sure that all of the gear that they would need for the camping trip was in order. He was glad that they had a shack on the far end of the ranch that was used by the ranch hands when the cattle and horses were in that area, and he hoped that it was in good shape. It was almost ten by the time that he was getting back to the ranch house, and he was just I time to bump into Shania arriving at the house at a slow gallop.

"Ah, so you finally managed to wake up, I was just about to give you a call to find out if the trip was still on," Tom said, stopping by the terrace as she brought her horse to a stop and swung her leg over it as she got off, looking hot as usual in her riding pants and boots, and her Stetson pulled low over her face to fend off the morning sunlight.

"I feel like hell, but I can manage, how about you, I thought that you had the most to drink back there and yet you look so fresh," she said as he walked over to her and hugged her warmly, one of the ranch hands taking her horse away.

"Coffee and a cold shower always do the trick for me, come on in, we had better check if Daniel is still asleep, he was dead when I left here an hour ago," Tom said, putting his hand over the small of her back as he led her into the house.

"You should have watched his drinking, silly, what if he is too tired to go with us?" she jokingly punched her fist into his side.

"I'll gladly take you there myself and share you with nobody all weekend long," he could feel the excitement within her as they made their way up the stairs to the bedroom he shared with Daniel.

He pushed the door open, and Daniel was just coming out of the bathroom, a huge erection on his crotch, and Tom noted the way that Shania looked at it longingly, just the same way that she looked at his, the fire in her eyes building up instantly as she swallowed hard. Tom even sensed the way that her breathing caught in her throat, her irises dilating with desire.

"Morning guys, and hey you pretty lady, you seem mesmerized by my cock, surprised to see that I have an erection?" he said tossing his towel onto the bed and turning to look at her.

Tom also felt a surge of arousal looking at the cock that brought him so much pleasure, and he felt the blood within his veins beginning to get hot. He felt his dick shifting around in his Jean's, and he had to fight the urge to get down on his knees and take Danny's dark erection into his mouth, sucking on it until Daniel groaned with delight as he came in his mouth.

"Better get dressed, Daniel, we have a few hours of horseback to do before we reach the far end of the ranch, remember," he said, as he forced himself to look away from him.

"Tom is right, Danny, better hurry up," Shania said moving over to him and kissing him lightly on the cheek before moving quickly away from him before temptation took over and she did what she wanted.

"Alright, I'll be ready within ten minutes," Danny said, stroking his cock up and down for their convenience, and Tom had to wrap his hand around Shania's waist and led her out of the room before any of them were tempted to do something that could possibly put off their trip.

"Wow, you guys both look better and better every single time that I lay my eyes on you, and I can't believe just how aroused seeing Daniel naked has made me," she breathed heavily, and he could tell the way that her heart was beating wildly in her chest as she trembled under his touch.

"Don't you worry, sweetheart, there will be plenty of time for that during the camping trip, and I'm not very sure if you will be able to handle us both all weekend," Tom said, fighting his own desire and changing his mind to tune to the trip that they were about to embark on.

Sophia had packed their food baskets and Tom had one of the farm hands put it away on one of the horses that were to carry their luggage. The three lovers were soon ready to leave for their camping trip, and they got onto their horses. A farm hand had already gone before them with the horses carrying what they would need for the trip, and also so that he could clean the shack where they were to sleep and ensure that there was plenty of firewood and fresh water there. Tom pulled the brim of his Stetson over his eyes as he steered the horse over the prairie. It took them a few hours on horseback, stopping a couple of times to let the horses drink and rest for a while as they ate a snack. The sun was setting by the time that they got to the site where they would be spending the weekend, and they were all pretty exhausted and sweaty. The ranch hand had delivered everything and was nowhere to be found. He had probably gone and pitched a tent somewhere in the bush.

"What a pity we arrived too late to go out hunting," Daniel said, "it would have been pretty interesting hunting down deer and then making some barbeque out of it."

"Really, do you guys hunt while you are out here, I've always wanted to do that, but I never got the chance because nobody at home ever wanted to go out hunting with a woman?" Shania said, almost with a hint of envy.

"Well, then, this is your lucky chance, because tomorrow after inspecting the ranch, we could ride into the mountain for some deer hunting, honey. Now, in the meantime, we had better get a fire going before it gets too cold," Tom said after they had secured the horses and were making their way into the shack.

"I think what I really need is a shower and then a drink," I feel like hell," Shania said, removing her riding jacket and tossing it onto a chair.

"There is a shower out in the back of the shack, but you might have to wait for the water to heat up," Danny said, going out to start gather the firewood at a gazebo outside the shack.

They had a huge fire burning within no time, and while Shania went into the shower for a bath, Tom and Daniel opted to go and bathe at a stream that was near the shack, since they felt dirty and the need for a lot of water. By the time that they got back to the camp site, Shania was seated in the gazebo by the bonfire, but that was not what caught Tom and Danny's eyes, she had laid her towel on the ground next to the fire and was lying naked on it with a glass of whiskey in her hand, the flames from the fire reflecting over her body in the sexiest way possible.

"Oh my goodness, Tom, doesn't she look divine?" Danny asked as they stopped in their tracks and looked at her sexy body.

"She looks like the sex goddess," Tom said as his body fed her beauty, feeling it setting off something within him, something that Shania always managed to do.

"You know what, Tom, I think I'm in love with her too, there is just this really strange feeling that I have been having within me over the last couple of days, a feeling that I have tried to push to the back of my mind, but it just won't go away. I think I have feeling for her, just the way that I have feelings for you, honey," Daniel said, and Tom could tell that it had taken a lot of thinking and bravery for him to tell him that.

"Really?" Tom asked in disbelief, as the reality of what Valerie had told him sunk in. he also decided that it was time that he confessed his real feelings. "I have had the same exact feelings but just didn't know how to go about them. I was feeling sort of guilty for being in love with two people at the same time, you and Shania, but there is no denying it now, whenever I'm with either or both of you, I feel like my heart is at it's happiest. Do you think that is a normal thing, I mean, it is very hard to come across a love triangle like this one that we share, that is, if Shania feels the same way about us."

"From the way that she looks at both of us, I'm beginning to think that the two men that she was talking about the other day by the river must be us, I think that we are the two men that she is in love with, and that is why she is so selfless and uninhibited when she is with us," Danny said.

"Come on, we had better get some dinner fixed, and then maybe we can confront her to tell us what she feels," Tom said, the thought of what the reality might be making his dick shift around in his pants.

They went into the house and heated the food that Sophia had packed for them on the kerosene stove. They then made their way out of the shack with the food and more bottles of whiskey.

"I was wondering what time you were coming back from the river, I'm starving," Shania said, sitting up on her elbow and draining her drink, before squinting at them. "No, no, no, not fair at all, you guys have to take your clothes off like me."

"That shouldn't be a problem at all, but first, you need to eat something," Tom's dick was already hard as he handed her a plate of rice and beef stew.

CHAPTER 47

The alcohol had already gotten to her head as she took the plate of food from Tom and sat upright to eat. She felt light headed in a good way, an exciting way, actually, because she was with the only two people that mattered in her heart right now, and as she delved into her food, she could see them both removing their clothes through the corners of her eyes, the most erotic sight as the flames from the fire shone on the dark and light skinned bodies. She realized how hungry she was as she spooned down all the food on the plate, and by the time she was done she felt much better.

"You guys seem relatively quiet, what's up," she said, getting up and placing her plate on a table, before taking her glass and refilling it with whiskey although she was not one of a very strong whiskey person.

"Hungry, tired and horny," Danny said, leaning on his back on a mat as Tom adjusted the fire, and she noted the way that both men had huge delicious looking erections that looked like they needed some attention.

"Now, that is what I'm talking about, I've been feeling horny from the time I was riding my horse with the saddle rubbing over my pussy," she said, taking a swig of her drink and loving the way that it burned a trail through her stomach and her intestines, sending a wave of pleasure all the way down to her clit, which felt good in the glare of the heat from the bonfire.

As she sat back down on her towel, Tom came and crouched down infront of her, parting her thighs after he drained his whiskey. Shania closed her eyes as he dipped his head in between her thighs, his lips closing over her pussy lips as he ran his tongue through her slick horny folds. She bucked her hips so that her cunt could connect harder with his mouth and opened her eyes to look at the way that he was lapping at her cunt, moving his tongue deliciously up and down her inner pussy lips. The tongue kept rubbing over her clit, giving her sensations that she knew she would never be able to forget. As she lost herself in the erotic pleasure that Tom was giving her, she watched Danny move behind Tom, making him get onto his hands and knees, his eyes fiery with desire.

Danny took his hands down to Tom's buttocks and parted the butt cheeks wide, before he lowered his head down and ran his tongue down and up the butt crack. An intense desire coursed through Shania's body as she watched something that many women would have paid top dollar to watch. Danny's tongue disappeared into Tom's butt hole as he licked and poked him, and from the look on Danny's face, and the heavy breathing of Tom's breath in her cunt, she could tell that both men were really enjoying themselves. Danny then moved away from Tom's butt and came forward, his dark hands pulling Tom's face away from her cunt. She felt his fingers probing her cunt, driving deep into her, before he pulled out and moved back behind Tom, as Tom resumed eating out her vagina.

Danny spread the pussy juices from her cunt over Tom's butt hole, and Shania felt the heat within her folds soaring when she saw Daniel taking a hold of his cock and guiding it into Tom's ass hole. He had a priceless look on his face as he pushed his dick into Tom's butt hole slowly, driving it all the way in to the hilt, and reminding her of how she had felt when her own ass was reamed the other day. She watched as Daniel began moving his dick in and out of Tom's butt hole, slowly at first, and then faster and harder with each stroke, feeling as if it was her own cunt or butt being fucked. She could feel Tom moaning in her cunt heatedly, and at one point he even bit her clit lightly, the pain sending a pleasurable feel through her body. Daniel gripped Tom by the hips and soon she could see his crotch slapping against Tom's butt.

The sex that they were having was so intense, more intense than it would ever be with a woman, and Shania found herself blown away by their desire, the heat within her cunt heightening with every stroke of the chocolate cock in Tom's ass. A million different expressions formed on Danny's face, and she translated that to a million different feeling of pleasure he was feeling with the tightness of Tom's butt over his dick. Daniel lifted a hand and spanked Tom's butt cheek, the spot that he slapped coloring and Shania felt the intensity of the pleasure that Tom was feeling. He sucked her clit into his mouth and began sucking hard on it as he drove a finger into the depths of her love nest, beginning to finger fuck her pleasurably. This was all too much for her, and Shania felt as if she could not breathe. The pleasure that she was feeling almost felt surreal and she hoped that it was not just some dream that would come to an end and bring her back to reality with a deep sense of need within her.

"Oh fuck, Tom, I'm coming," Danny grunted as he pushed his dick deep into Tom's butt, shooting his load of desire into his butt hole, just as Shania also lost it, her world spinning around in circles as her climax rocked her hard and intensely.

Her cunt quaked over the finger within her as she creamed up with the juices of her passion, watching as some of Daniel's semen gushed out of the sides of Tom's butt hole, both of them coming intensely. She felt an intense pleasure and a sudden need to be filled, she needed one of her lover's to fill her up with his thickness and make her feel whole, make her feel part of the love triangle that they were. She knew that Tom was also dying for his release since she could see that his cock was as hard as a rock as he moved his mouth away from her cunt and got up.

"Tom, please fuck me, fuck me real nice and hard, fuck, I'm in love with both of you men, make me yours right now, let us all become one, a trio in love, because I have the feeling that you feel the same way," Shania said, without thinking, and revealing her deepest secret without realizing it, because of all the passion she felt.

"Wha-" Tom began before she cunt him short.

"Just fuck me, Tom, please, we will talk during the afterglow," she said urgently as she pushed Daniel seated on the mat and got onto her hands and knees before him, lowering her head down to his cum stained cock that smelled of male sex, an arousing scent that made her dizzy with desire.

She took the soft cock in her mouth and began swishing it around in her mouth as she licked off the mess of the male love making, and actually finding that she liked the taste. She took the whole of the limp cock into her mouth and began sucking on it as she massaged the balls, while Tom moved behind her. She felt Tom parting her thighs slightly, and then he ran his fingers through her cunt as she trembled with desire. He drove a finger deep into her folds, rubbing it over her G spot as he pulled out, and Shania moaned onto the dick in her mouth, the pleasure vibrating through her body and yet his dick had not even entered her. As Tom pulled the finger out of her cunt, Shania braced herself, holding her breath when she felt his dick brushing over her butt cheek. Tom guided his deliciousness into her, slamming it in hard and driving it in all the way to the hilt as she moaned onto the cock in her mouth.

Tom let his dick stay lodged deep in her cunt as she recovered from the sensations of the hard entry, and she felt him parting her butt cheeks. A finger joined his dick in her cunt, and as if pulled out and skidded through the sensitive patch of skin between her pussy and her anus, Shania once again felt herself holding her breath. The finger pushed into the rim of her butt hole just as Tom began fucking her hard and fast, the pleasure within her body making her weak with desire. She surrendered to the lovers of her life as Tom fucked her hard and fast, harder than he had ever fucked her before, and she found herself enjoying every moment of it. She loved the feel of his dick within her, and as it drove into her, she could feel it hitting over her uterus, reminding her of just how deep it was going inside her folds.

The cock in her mouth had already begun hardening in her mouth, and it was a pleasant feel, a dick hardening in her mouth. the thought that it might also bone her as soon as Tom was done with her made her feel wildly aroused, heightening the pleasure within her folds as she accommodated Tom's dick, massaging it with her pussy walls deliciously. Once again she felt an overwhelming heat beginning to form within her folds and she knew that she would soon be seeing the stars as she climaxed. The cock in her mouth was soon fully blown, and her head began bobbing up and won on it as she mouth fucked Danny. He took his hands down to her head, pressing it harder onto his dick and forcing more of the male meat into her mouth. the thickness of the black monster cock stretched her jaws painfully, but she was determined to take as much of it into her mouth as she could.

As Tom boned her, Shania could feel his dick rubbing over his finger though the thin tissues that separated the two love holes, making her feel every digit on the finger and every vein in his dick. She closed her eyes and concentrated on the erotic pleasure that she felt. Tom shagged her harder than ever, and it was not long before she climaxed hard, her world revolving around the intense pleasure that she felt within her folds as every erotic nerve in her body came alive with her desire. Tom continued hammering his cock in and out of her cunt, riding her orgasm off, and just when she was beginning to wonder if he would come, he pulled his dick out of her pussy, dipping it into her butt hole hard as he shot his hot load of semen within her. Still reeling from the effects of the orgasm in her butt, she did not expect the huge load of cum that suddenly erupted in her mouth as Danny climaxed. She gripped the base of his dick, jerking it furiously as she struggled to swallow every drop of semen that shot out of his love pipe.

CHAPTER 48

When Shania woke up, she realized that she was on a small bed and was sandwiched between Tom and Danny. When she opened her eyes, she found her head nuzzled in Danny's chest and could feel his dick hard against her thigh. Behind her, in her butt crack, she could feel Tom's hard length pulsating, and it made her wonder how they could wake up with hard ons like this after all of the wild love making they'd had, both outside the shack, and inside. Her butt and pussy still felt sore from the intense pounding, and she also realized that her jaw felt sore from blowing cock for too long. Both men seemed to be sound asleep, and wondering what time it was, she silently got out of the bed. A sick feeling hit her stomach before she could do anything, and she ran to the bathroom and retched her retched her intestines out. She felt dizzy and sickly as she sat with her head leaning over the toilet bowl. She got up and rinsed her mouth, still feeling a little dizzy, but her stomach feeling much better. When she turned to get out of the bathroom, she bumped into a huge mass that she recognized instantly.

"Are you okay?" Tom asked, holding her firm as she almost lost her balance.

"Yeah, I probably had a little too much to drink, but I feel much better now, thanks," she said, her eyes travelling over his body and resting on his dick, which trembled with renewed desire.

Tom's mind raced. The symptoms that she had just shown were not from a hangover, they were symptoms that were exhibited by women in their early weeks of pregnancy. It suddenly downed on him that either Danny or he were responsible for it, and the thought excited him in a strange way, they were going to be parents, all three of them. To him it did not matter if it was his or Danny's, all that mattered was the love that they all shared.

"Tom, why are you staring at me like that?" her eyes slowly moved back to his from his dick.

"How often do you get this sort of hangover in the morning?" he asked.

"I've had this feeling maybe twice or thrice, why, why do you ask, is there something wrong with a hangover?" she asked, definitely having no idea that she was pregnant.

"Shania, honey, that is not a hangover," he smiled at her. "You are pregnant, you, Danny and I are going to be parents, can you believe that?"

Her hands flew to her mouth, her eyes clouding with fear at first, before a glow lit up within them as she looked at him as if she could not believe what he was telling her. She threw her hands around him, hugging him tightly as if she was holding on for dear life.

"What did you just say, honey, are you sure about that?" she squealed, her excitement evident in her voice. "Am I really pregnant? What did you mean by the three of us being parents? Please tell me that I am not dreaming, Tom, tell me the truth, am I pregnant?"

"Morning, and what are you two talking about here?" Daniel's huge frame filled the doorway as he stood there looking at them questioningly.

"Danny, Shania, you and I are gonna be parents," Tom said, unable to hold back the urge to hug Daniel as he threw his hands around him and hugged him tightly. "Shania is pregnant for us."

"What?" was all that Danny managed to say as he pushed Tom aside and hugged Shania, placing his hand on her belly and rubbing it over it softly and protectively. "Thank you, Shania, this is the best gift that you could have brought into our lives, and especially if what you meant about being madly in love with us last night is true."

She nodded at him, tears of joy rolling down her cheeks when she realized that both of the men were also in love with her and willing for the three of them to be like family, lover's and parents without caring whose baby was in her womb, although she could still hardly believe it, although she had suspected it the first time she got morning sickness, since she had not been drinking the night before. The reality of the situation began to down on her, and she found herself beginning to panic. What the hell would she tell her parents and brothers? It would have been better if she had known who the father of the child was amongst the two, but she had no idea whether it was Tom or Daniel.

"Here is what we are going to do," Daniel said, as if reading her mind and sensing her dilemma. "We need to arrange a wedding as soon as possible, before anyone else at your place notices that you are pregnant."

"Excellent idea, but since when does the law permit a woman to get married to two husbands at the same time?" she said to him as the three of them walked back into the bedroom.

"Officially, you can get married to me, but unofficially, you will be married to both of us, and we will be one happy trio in love and expecting a baby, irrespective of who the biological father is," Tom said quickly, heading for his pants and sweeping out his cell phone to call Valerie, so that Valerie could start making the necessary arrangements as excitement filled them all.

CHAPTER 49

"Push, Valerie, push," the doctor said, looking in between her thighs as she held onto Tom with one hand and Danny with the other, pushing harder as cramps of pain tore through her.

Suddenly there was the sound of a baby crying and she laid back in relief as the ordeal of giving birth came to an end. She raised her sweat laden head slightly and looked at the baby, whom the doctor wrapped in a towel.

"It is a baby boy, congratulations, Mr. and Mrs. Sharpe," the doctor said, looking at the whole group, although he could not seem to understand what Daniel was also doing in the room.

Tears of joy filled their eyes as Tom took the little bundle of joy from the doctor and looked at him, before handing him to Danny, who then handed the baby to the mother. As the doctor exited the room, Valerie and Sophia walked into the room, tears of joy also rolling down their cheeks. Valerie winked at Tom, and Tom could see the happiness he felt at seeing his son.

"I am so proud of all of you, and thank you for this new member of our family, what is his name?" Valerie asked, taking the baby from the mother and tickling his cheeks with a finger as the three lover's looked at each other, realizing that they had not yet settled on a name for the baby. "I know what we can call him, we will call him Danny Sharpe IV, how does that sound, it combines the love that we all feel for each other as a family."

"We love the name," Shania said on behalf of herself and both of her husband's. "Thank you Valerie."

Baby Danny lay in his crib fast asleep. He was now six months old and the heart of everyone at the mansion. Tom, Daniel and Shania lay on the huge bed, and he held Shania with his morning erection resting inside her pussy from behind, spooning her, while Tom was behind him, his cock also hard, but still inside Tom's butt hole, where it had been when they had fallen asleep. Who would have thought that their lives would have ended up being like this, so happy, so close and better lovers than they had ever been. He moved his dick slightly inside Shania's cunt and he felt her responding when she felt his cock deep inside her, shifting her butt in such a way that his cock settled even deeper in her pussy, the warmth of her cunt over his cock as delicious as it had been the first time that he had fucked her, breaking her virginity. Behind him, he felt Daniel put his hand on his hips, holding him still as he forced his dick deeper into his butt hole, the thick dark cock harder and stealthier than ever. He drifted back to sleep, a smile on his face.

ABOUT THE AUTHOR

Jodie Sloan loves reading and writing romance stories. Her love for romance began when she had started reading romance stories and grown to love them more as she started writing.

Her passion for writing has motivated her to write several book series of her own. Currently, Jodie Sloan is in the process of writing several more book series that she hopes will be worth reading.

She cherishes her family and takes each day as an opportunity to love, read and write.

Jodie loves to hear your feedback, reach her through:

Facebook

https://www.facebook.com/pages/JodieSloan/180879798753822

Get Future New Releases In This Series For 99 Cents

http://eepurl.com/7jckT

Printed in Great Britain
by Amazon